KINGDOM OF ARTHUR

—BOOK FIVE—
THE LADY IN THE LAKE

© 2018

MATTHEW L. MARTIN

THE LADY IN THE LAKE

novels | shorts | poems
news about upcoming books
booksbymatthew.com

MATTHEW L. MARTIN

THE SIX-PART KINGDOM OF ARTHUR BOOK SERIES...

   I   THE ILL-WINDS OF FATE
   II   THE HEADWINDS OF DESTINY

※※※※※

   III   THE QUEST OF SIR LANCELOT
   IV   THE MAN WITH TWO FACES

※※※※※

   V   THE LADY IN THE LAKE
   VI   THE DEATH OF ARTHUR

THE LADY IN THE LAKE

CONTENTS

p009 – PROLOGUE

p043 – (chapter 1)
AGAINST PROTOCOL

p059 – (chapter 2)
RABBLE

p077 – (chapter 3)
THE ILL-MADE KING

p099 – (chapter 4)
SURPRISE

p111 – (chapter 5)
LEAVE NO DOUBT

p127 – (chapter 6)
THE WIZARD AND THE CROOK

p151 – (chapter 7)
FATHER AND SONS

p163 – (chapter 8)
FALLEN KINGDOM

MATTHEW L. MARTIN

CONTENTS

p181 – (chapter 9)
REVELATION

p201 – (chapter 10)
MOTHER AND SON

p219 – (chapter 11)
GENIE IN A BOTTLE

p237 – (chapter 12)
ABSOLUTION AND RESOLUTION

p251 – (chapter 13)
A TURKISH WHIRLWIND

p269 – (chapter 14)
SECOND-BORN

p291 – (chapter 15)
THE LADY AND THE LAKE

p305 – appendices

p364 – acknowledgements

p365 – dedication

THE LADY IN THE LAKE

MATTHEW L. MARTIN

Stories come
and stories go,
telling tales
for men to know;
tales of heroes
with great renown,
and lesser ones who wore no crown; of those who fight
to stem the tide, and those who seek for souls to die.
A victory is
drawing near,
but who'll prevail
is not yet clear.
The dead are stirring,
soon to wake;
the hero's call
must ring.
Hopeful eyes
turn to England,
and to her
ill-made king...

THE LADY IN THE LAKE

Prologue

Ages ago, before they were called Turks, the WuStyni were a savage and uncultured people, quick to hatred and swift to kill. Scattered across the lands far to the east of Mesopotamia, the people hunted and gathered, mated and killed, grouped into clans and then warred amongst themselves. Chaos ruled their lands. Without language or art to unite them or enlighten them, their region was perpetually consumed by war, death and ruin.

Then the sand serpents came.

Awesome in their length, the greatest of them could stretch the span of five men. They slithered

THE LADY IN THE LAKE

out of the mountains, east of their borders, and feasted on the lives of those who dared to challenge them. Many tried to slay the creatures, hoping for the glory that comes with such a kill, but none could do it. Fighting them brought the WuStynni clans together but the creatures were too great and too strong, and when threatened would burrow into the earth, to multiply and grow, only to emerge stronger and deadlier months later.

The people fled to the mountains to escape them, digging tunnels and caves. They cut through the rock to make passages to traverse without venturing into the open air, but the snakes grew restless, hungry and numerous. They slithered out of their desert homes and into the caves, trapping the WuStynni and consuming them whole. Eventually the people were dwindled down to only a thousand or so, constantly fleeing the predator-serpents.

Then the Merkall came.

That's what they called him, anyway. He never told them his real name, but they called him "Merkall WuStyn chokang," which, in their tongue, means "the man who does secret things." The secret-doer appeared from the east one day, small in frame, dark skinned and clutching his walking stick. There was age to him, it was obvious, despite a young face; he **seemed** much older than everyone else. Perhaps it was his eyes:

MATTHEW L. MARTIN

His yellow eyes carried much wisdom. His black robe soaked up the sun, but his shiny bald head seemed to sparkle in the light. He walked with a purpose across the sunny terrain, toward the mountain caves where the people were hiding. Inside, his yellow eyes shone in the dark, lighting the way to a family clustered and terrified, down to their last scraps of food.

"Where are the creatures now?" he asked a little girl, ignoring the panicked pleas for help from her parents. The girl pointed down a long dark tunnel. When Merkall looked, his beaming yellow eyes illuminated the path, causing a shadow to stir and move away. Without speaking, he moved toward it, disappearing around the corner while the family waited and listened.

There was a flash, then a wail and the whiff of charred flesh wafted down the alleyway. Merkall returned a moment later, his staff smoking like it had just been on fire. His eyes dimmed and appeared normal again. "You will help me climb the mountain above." he said to the little girl's father. The man stood up, towering over the smaller wizard, and nodded in deference and gratitude.

There was no easy path to the top. The mountains in the east were jagged spires that pierced the heavens. You could not walk up them; you had to climb with hands and feet, clutching at rocky outcroppings, hoping they would support

THE LADY IN THE LAKE

your weight. The air was colder, and a fog lingered, thick in the air. They climbed as high as any man could, with only a lone peak left unscaled, too small to bother with.

Yet Merkall bothered.

He handed his walking stick to his companion, and climbed up the remaining spire, wrapping his arms and legs around it like a cat climbing a tree. At the peak, he called for his staff to be tossed to him and when he caught it, he plunged it into the side of the spire.

The mountain below rumbled. The whole world seemed to shake, in fact. Merkall watched, gazing over the fog to the desert below, where movement was shifting along the ground. From the mountain's peak it looked like tan and silver strands were wiggling out of the bottom of the mountain. A dozen, a dozen-dozen, then hundreds more poured out of the caves and cracks, sand serpents burrowing under the gentle terrain of the valley below.

Merkall climbed down the mountain's spire, down the mountain's peak, down the mountain's path and down the mountain's foot, finally reaching the edge of the valley. The soft ground rippled with activity under the surface. He watched it for a moment while WuStyni crept out of their caves to watch **him**.

A sand serpent erupted from the earth,

opening its vast mouth as it turned to dive toward the small bald man, its jaws spread wide enough to swallow the wizard whole. Merkall lifted his staff toward it, however, and sent a beam of sunlight crashing into it like a tidal wave. The creature was knocked back onto the shifting ground as other snakes coiled around their fallen brother, hissing and spitting threats at the one who defied them.

Merkall raised his staff once more, sending the creatures scurrying away from the obvious danger. He thrust his walking stick into the soft ground; the shockwave that resulted was tremendous, sending chunks of earth, grass and rocks flying into the sky. For a moment the man was standing in a crater that had only just formed, with silver and tan serpentine bodies flying into the air from the impact.

The debris fell back to the earth, and with a dramatic wave of his staff, Merkall put the soil back to how it'd been before. The snakes slithered away, however; out of the sand, away from the mountains and toward the deserts east of the land. Merkall turned around to see scores of WuStyni watching him silently.

"The east is dangerous," he said to those who gathered nearby. His meek voice lacked even a hint of the deep baritone that accompanied the voice of WuStyni men, yet he held their attention so entirely it was like he was whispering into each

THE LADY IN THE LAKE

of their ears. "I suggest you build to the west." He walked away after that, back toward the east from whence he'd come.

He was never seen again.

*****

Centuries passed and the legend of the Merkall faded from memory and teaching. In time the WuStyni clans grew larger and more violent, as they were before the sand serpents came. Each clan taught their children that their clan's leader was the descendant of the one who drove the sand serpents away (while the other clans merely watched, they would say, helpless and weak).

Fighting between the lands was endless. As soon as one clan became large enough to encroach on another's territory they were ransacked, plundered, raped and killed. The brief time when the people united to fight—and later to flee—the sand snakes was long gone. None of the various clans ever went long before they were raided by a neighboring clan, and those clan leaders who tried to avoid such raids were killed by their own, as the people saw a lack of bloodlust as a weakness to be exploited.

Boys were raised to hunt and kill, girls were raised to breed. The cycle of barbarism continued long after the other regions of the known world evolved and established true civilizations,

MATTHEW L. MARTIN

Lordships, kingdoms, and more. While the Old Lands and the Norse Lands developed culture, traditions and basic decency (despite their own wars and such), the WuStyni remained locked in brutality and an animal-like disregard for life.

The most prosperous clan was in the heart of their region, at the edge of a great river that flowed south, with palm trees and plant life growing abundantly. Here, all who pledged their life to the River Clan lived plentifully and prosperously.

SenTot ruled this land. He was the oldest clan-leader of them all, and the most brutal. Quick to kill anyone he thought might pose a threat or who did not show proper deference toward him, SenTot seized the River Clan from his uncle, PorKal after he refused to take blood-vengeance on a clan-leader that killed his daughter. PorKal had grown complacent and comfortable, afraid to engage an enemy and risk losing the pleasant life he'd built for himself.

Some clan-leaders were gangly, thin and starving, traveling from land to land, scavenging and killing to survive. Other clan-leaders were fat and relaxed, relying on subordinates to do their work for them, and leaning on well-compensated guards to protect them. SenTot on the other hand was muscular, young and vibrant as much as he was ruthless and aggressive. He relished the opportunity to strike at an enemy, believing that every kill fed his starving soul, strengthening him

THE LADY IN THE LAKE

for the next challenge.

Women were scarce in those days. A clan-leader would kill any girl that was not born of his blood. Only his daughters could live and they were sold and pawned off as needed to keep his power intact. The value of a clan-leader's daughter was greatest in the land; securing one through gift, murder or thievery would be enough to buy one's way into a clan-leadership.

SenTot and his wife MadSu—whom he'd stolen as a child years before—had birthed four children, two girls and, later, twin-boys. The girls were quickly sold off to rivals to end a dispute between them: SenTot did not just fight his enemies, he often brokered peace between **other** enemies, to ensure neighboring clans did not fight and conquer and grow and become a threat to him.

His twin-boys were a different matter, however.

WuStyni believed that only the strongest man should rule, and once sons in a house came of age the father would determine which was stronger, killing the other. MadSu had tried to hide her second born son from SenTot, but the servant who helped her give birth betrayed her, revealing to him a strong and healthy first-born and a smaller, misshapen second-son. MadSu begged for the boys—both children—to be spared.

"Let them both grow!" she begged, pleading

on her knees to her husband. "Let them both grow as is our way and **then** determine who is strongest." She had hoped he'd be dead by the time the choice would need to be made, but he knew the moment he saw the stunted child which son was weak. The servant handed the child over without concern and SenTot bashed his head against the stone wall.

MadSu wept throughout the night.

In the morning her husband arose to leave, to kill a clan that had moved into his land. He came to her (as he often did before leaving on a hunt) but she resisted him, crippled by the death of her son. He forced himself upon her as was his way and left satisfied.

SenTot returned that evening, tired from battle and stained with the blood of his fallen enemies. He awoke late in the night to find his wife eager to satisfy him. He allowed her, and while she did, she plunged a knife into his ear.

She searched through the tents surrounding her own, looking for the servant who had happily given her child away to be killed. She found her in the tent of a warrior man, pleasuring him. She killed her with a stab to the back and when he climbed off the bed to attack her, she slit his throat, leaving them both bleeding in a heap on the ground.

She stared at the pool of blood as it seeped

THE LADY IN THE LAKE

into the earthy floor beneath her feet. The splatter had stained her face and hands, her eyes were stinging and her vision was blurred with a red tinge as blood dripped from the tip of her blade. This was no longer an act of vengeance. This was an awakening. She exited the tent, moving silently in the night. Two-dozen tents surrounded SenTot's and dozens more formed the perimeter of their clan. Purposefully, she slipped from tent to tent, killing men.

When the morning broke, not a single husband, man or son who had aged beyond childhood was left to kill.

The cries of women filled the morning air. One by one they all staggered out of their tents, whose openings faced the middle of the camp, where SenTot's tent was located. MadSu stood in the midst of them, her clothes and skin still stained with crimson blood, the knife she'd used to kill a hundred men in their sleep still held tight in her left hand.

She looked around to her confused and distraught peers. Many of them were covered in the blood of their men too. Their faces streaked from the tears they'd been shedding. "Cry!" she shouted to them. "Cry aloud and let the mountains shake with your grief! Cry loud and pained!" She tossed the knife down, stabbing the earth next to her foot. "But this morning will be the last time you cry over the death of any man. When the sun rises high, we will be WuStyn A'ma Turk" (which roughly translates from their language as "the people who do not cry").

A woman with a blood-stain on her lap—where the dying head of a loved one had rested—rushed toward her, screaming in rage and fury. She had no weapon, but MadSu did not pick up her own. She merely grabbed the woman, spun her around and wrapped her arms across her chest. The attacker did not even try to fight; she just continued sobbing. MadSu released her and she crumpled to the ground.

"What is your name?" she asked, feeling the eyes of everyone upon her.

"Riboora." The woman said, gently rubbing her fingers across the blood stain.

"Your son?" she asked, wondering which man she mourned so terribly. The woman nodded.

"He was no child." MadSu said. "He was a man who would soon enough rise to challenge for his own clan. To kill and take his own woman. To do with her whatever he wanted and to kill of hers whatever he desired."

She stepped away from the sobbing woman, moving slowly around the great tent of SenTot, making sure all the surrounding women could hear her voice. "Soon the morning will break again and you will stand over the bodies of men as many as the stars at night. They will all lie dead and bleeding at your feet. But you will not cry for them. The only cries you hear will be **from** them, as they beg you for mercy."

Riboora crawled back to her tent, resting against it. MadSu picked up her knife once more, caked with earth and blood. "Their women will rise and weep, and we will tell them what I am telling you. They will stop their crying. They will rise up and they will join us. And we will go, from clan to clan, reaping what our men long ago have sown."

A woman stepped forward, holding a knife of her own. She had first exited her tent intending to kill MadSu but the need for vengeance for the murder of the man who had killed her father, raped her mother and stolen her from her home was so faint and fleeting it disappeared without even a passing thought. She instead called out to her new leader. "The other clans will be coming. The clan north of us, who claim the river as their own will be coming."

MadSu turned to face her. "Yes, when the others hear what has been done they will come to claim this land and claim you for their own."

"Then you have killed us all!" a sobbing woman cried out. "They will come and claim us and if we fight as you say they will cut out our tongues and cut open our throats!"

"They may," MadSu replied simply, "if we do not fight. If we fight we can kill them, as I have done. One hundred men of this clan killed by my hand. Together how many more can **we** kill?!"

"You killed sleeping men. They are coming for war!"

"No. They are coming to claim women and land and to them there is little difference. They will hear what happened here, yes. But what will they hear?" She moved from woman to woman, piercing them with her gaze. "What will they hear?" she asked again, lowering her voice to something gentler and encouraging.

A modest woman, stained with blood on her shoulder stepped forward. "A clan from the Dead Lands came." she said, thinking of the lie on the spot.

Another woman stepped forward. "There was a battle in the camp. They killed each other."

Little by little they pieced together the story, adding to it parts that seemed reasonable and believable, especially to a band of scavenging savages. A mother and two boys were sent up the river with a tale to tell.

The next day, when the sun was hot in the western sky, a clan from the Northern River Lands rode in. They entered the tents and slept with the women, and enjoyed a knife in their necks for their trouble. The next day a woman and her sons traveled east toward the desert lands, where clans were quick to believe that River Land clans had razed the fertile terrain of SenTot and left the weak

THE LADY IN THE LAKE

and worthless women to be claimed. When morning broke, the blood flowed from ther tents like ruby rivers.

With each clan's death, the women of the clan were found, secured, recruited and sent out, sending their luring messages to neighboring clans, drawing them in and running them through with cold, piercing steel. Like a swarm the women moved, spreading across the wild lands, gaining more and more of an army as they went. MadSu moved in the midst of the swarm, organizing, rallying, comforting, motivating.

"By now the clans in the far north of the river will know of us." she said to her traveling clan of men-killers. "As will the clans on the other side of the Dead Mountains. We have conquered half this land through cunning." She picked up her knife from the ground and holstered it at her hip. "The other half will be won in battle."

*****

The spectacle of MadSu's nomadic army was certainly grand. They were a massive rectangle of marchers—some soldiers, some servants—traversing like a herd across the Wild Lands. Their army cleared through the land, before turning north to purge those clans of their barbarian clan-leaders and men. They followed the river to the Northern Mountains, driving out the clans therein. The going was easier than she might have publicly stated, even with more and more clans being aware of the so-called "wild woman" and her "army of cattle."

Not all of her followers could fight; many were too old or too young, others simply too weak, but the ones who could wield a weapon often proved themselves more cunning and skillful than any man they faced. The clans' warriors may have been bigger and stronger but they fought with arrogance; her warriors fought with purpose, not with the presumption of victory but with the will to achieve it.

Her closest advisers were led by her "septle" (the WuStyni word for "sister"), ChavNu, whom she rescued while liberating a Storm Lands clan. The four of them—MadSu, ChavNu, Riboora, and Beckralla—remained close at all times, trusting no one else, confiding in no one else, and sleeping comfortably with no one else. The women of the WuStyni were not as treacherous and cruelly-ambitious as their male counterparts, but MadSu still wondered which of her followers wished to be leader in her place. The four leaders slept in the same tent, sleeping in two-by-two shifts. Nevertheless, over the course of a year, while she purged clan after clan and grew the number of her followers, no one risked an attack on her life.

One night, as the winter air in the mountains made the already-cool nights particularly frigid, a messenger burst into their tent. MadSu was

THE LADY IN THE LAKE

sharing the watch and nearly threw a knife through the woman's heart. The messenger was wide-eyed and panicked. "Come please, hurry!" was all she said before turning back out into the night.

They exited their tent, perched further up the mountain than the rest; perched high so the rest of her nation (as she'd started calling them) could be watched. There were a few fires peppering the landscape in between the tents but nothing looked unusual. They heard the scuffle of footfall on rocky soil and saw the panicked servant hurrying down the mountain.

"What is it?" MadSu called, but as the woman turned to answer she could only utter a grunt. At the same time a terrible thud-and-squish sound burst from the servant's location. She fell over, clutching the long spear that had been driven into her chest.

"Invaders!" Riboora said. They hurried back to their tent, seizing weapons, ready to fight whomever entered.

None did.

They heard movement outside but still none entered. "Cowards!" MadSu called out, but the sounds had stopped. Whoever had been outside had gone away, her challenge unheeded.

"Fire!" ChavNu called. Spinning around they saw the black smoke pouring in from the bottom of their tent. An orange glow rose like the sun over the smoke, eating away at the thick fabric. "There too!" she yelled, pointing at the opposite direction as the area began to fill with smoke. Beckralla made for the entrance, but MadSu's outstretched hand pulled her back. Silently she shook her head and beckoned for the quartet to cut through the back of the tent.

Outside, the heat of the flames was already filling the cold air around them. They peered around one side, watching as three men, with swords ready, stood near the front of the enclosure, ready to ambush them as they exited the tent's opening. Now was not the time for stealth. There wasn't enough space for the four of them to spread out, so they ran single-file, with MadSu in the lead. Her roar startled them and she easily batted away the nearest soldier's lazy sword-swing. He died quickly. The other landed and glancing blow at her shoulder but Beckralla cut him down in response. Another was waiting on the opposite side of the tent but he chose to flee.

"That one runs for aid." Riboora said, tracking his dark outline in the night.

"More are coming, if not already here." MadSu said. "Sound the alarm."

ChavNu hurried down the mountain while the remaining three scanned the scene below, looking for some clue as to the location of their invaders. "There!" Riboora said, pointing to a

THE LADY IN THE LAKE

torchlight on the edge of the camp that had just been snuffed out. A moment later a low-octave hornblow sent the camp into a frenzy.

Suddenly the air was flooded with noise, as the shadowy mass that Riboora had spotted poured into the heart of the camp. They could hear the swordplay from their elevated spot; MadSu did not need to tell them: They all scampered quickly down to join the fight.

MadSu's nation pushed the invaders back as the frigid night turned to a frosty day. By the time the sun had fully risen, her people had won; a host of men littered the streets between their tents. She walked through her mobile city, checking on her wounded, assuring her civilians and encouraging her warriors.

"MadSu!" ChavNu called as she ran to her. She was carrying strips of leather, each etched with different designs.

"They were of the Northern River Clans." MadSu said, examining the strips her septle's hand.

"Yes, but these are not the same markings." ChavNu pointed out. "These are of the clan west of the river…these of the clan east." The two sisters met each other's gaze, silently for a moment, each drawing the same conclusion at the same time.

"The men have finally united against us." MadSu said. "We've finally given them reason to stand together." she added with a laugh, plucking the strips from her sister's hand and holding them up for those gathered nearby to see. "Here is the proof of our conquest!" she said. "They can not defeat us clan by clan so they do this." She tossed the leather pieces to the ground. "They marry each other now that they can't marry us! And they think this will stop us?! This just makes our work easier! Gather your wounded, sharpen your blades. Tomorrow we ride to the River Lands of the north, where I will cut off the head of the man who leads them!"

They marched the next morning and throughout the day, stopping only to let the feeble among them rest and drink from the mountain streams. They slept near the foothills with extra watches and scouts patrolling the camp, but no one disturbed them. The next day, by noon, they came to the place where two smaller brooks—called the Father and Mother Rivers—flowed into one. Waiting for them on the fertile land was an army of men; not a clan's assortment of warriors and barbarians, the kind which MadSu and her nation had managed to subdue through sheer overwhelming number, but a sprawling mass of fighters, assembled from dozens of surrounding clans.

"Tek." MadSu said to her trio alongside her. In the center of the army of the River Clans was a tall, bronze, muscular man, gripping twin scimitars, pacing back and forth like a lion ready to

THE LADY IN THE LAKE

be fed.

"Now we know who brought the clans together." Beckralla said. "I wonder what he bribed the other clans' leaders with."

"What do you think?" MadSu said. "He bribed them with us. If we win they die. If they win…" She looked back at her army of liberated slave-women. "The number of our warriors outnumbers theirs, but not nearly by the numbers our women are used to. They've never faced an army so prepared before…and we are tired from the journey."

"Do not lose hope." Riboora said. "I do not see frightened girls behind us. I see warriors."

MadSu turned back to the army of men standing ready for their opponents to make the first move. Tek seemed to have found her with his eyes. He was now frozen, staring at her. She had the unshakeable feeling that this battle, no matter what happened, would come down to the two of them crossing swords. "Then let us go to war." she said, rushing with a roar toward the enemy opposite her. The rumble of those charging behind her and the rumble of those charging ahead of her seemed to shake the mountains and churn the rivers.

Swords clashed, limbs were cut and bodies fell dead. Her warriors fought true, and as it had gone so many times before, the arrogance of her enemy slowed them, dulled them and made them easy prey. She skirmished with half-a-dozen men, and despite a wounded shoulder, MadSu slew them all. Her women fought in pairs and trios, while many of the men refused to call for aid, certain they could put the challengers back in their places alone.

Her eye caught sight of Beckralla, cutting down a challenger as Tek approached from behind. She opened her mouth to call for her attention, but it was too late. By the time the sound had erupted from MadSu's stomach and burst out of her lips, the great wide blade was running through Beckralla's midsection, and her cry of warning became a cry of anguish.

Tek's eyes were on MadSu, paying Beckralla no mind as she fell to the ground, a bleeding mess. This was the moment, she knew. He tossed one of his swords down, clutching the other in both hands. Unlike his army, he was not going to overlook his opponent. They circled each other, while the chaos of war continued all around them. It washed away into a distant echo in her ears and a soft blur in her peripheral vision. He was all she saw. His footfall, scratching the dry ground, was all she heard.

And then a sword burst out of his chest.

Tek fell to the ground, a bleeding mess. In his place stood a fatter, uglier, lighter-skinned warrior, who paid her no mind while he chuckled at the

THE LADY IN THE LAKE

man he'd killed. "Looks like I **will** be leading your army after all." he said, kicking Tek's corpse with his leather-strapped foot. He finally noticed MadSu standing a few paces from him. "Stand aside girl, you've had your adventure but it's all done now."

"I am not a girl to be ordered. I am MadSu, the wild woman; liberator of the clans, slayer of men."

He laughed a great belly laugh, sincerely enjoying what he'd just heard. "Are you really? Of course you are. Look at you. You've got more spunk than all these other girls. Do you know what I am—what **he** and I both are?" he said, pointing his sword at Tek's body. "We're your sons!"

She did not respond though she wondered how he would know about her sons and what game he was playing by invoking them like this. She also quickly wondered about her living son, if he was still safe with the others in the mountain above."

His laughter recaptured her attention. "I'm serious. We're your sons. Not by birth of course..." he grinned a nasty yellow smile. "Not that I wouldn't mind having a peak down there. Nah we're your boys by marriage. That husband of yours sold his girls off to us to be wed when they were old enough. They were only a year or so when we got em, but they was a pretty prize already and in a few years woulda been worth a bit of spoiling."

MadSu was shaking now.

"Once we got wind of your adventure Tek wanted us to keep the girls to barter with." He stuck his blood-stained sword in his mouth and began picking his teeth with it. "But I figured negotiating with a bunch of women was a fool's game, and the girls'd be more trouble'n they was worth anyway, so when he came out here to look all intimidating I went to where he was keeping them and…" He ran the dull side of his blade across his throat, making a face that mocked a dead man.

What happened next was between MadSu and the man who told her this terrible story. She killed him, obviously, but she never shared the details with anyone, not even her sister. In fact, later on, whenever she would be asked if she ever found her daughters as she'd found ChavNu, she would only reply that she'd received word they'd been killed, but left the details vague. For some reason (a reason she could not explain to herself), she felt like the details needed to be kept privately within herself.

She did however parade around the head of the man who'd killed her children, having never bothered to learn his name. And for good measure she cut off the head of Tek as well. Even the men

THE LADY IN THE LAKE

who saw her wandering the battlefield, with a head in each hand, kept their distance from her; she was covered almost head to toe in blood, with a dazed look in her eye. She sat down against a tent as the rest of the battle unfolded.

The clans of men had poor organization and were quick to abandon one another or refuse to aid each other in distress. Her army, on the other hand, fought with singular purpose, singular focus and singular intensity. As the sun turned red in the western sky, the stragglers that remained quickly scattered and MadSu's warriors stepped through the cloud of agitated dust and dirt a victorious army.

After sweeping the northern clans and freeing their women and children, the nation rested, with some wondering if their work was finished.

"It is not." MadSu answered, sitting under a palm tree and staring off toward the south. "The River Lands are ours, the Storm Lands are ours, but the south...beyond the Dead Mountains have yet to be taken."

"You know who dwells beyond the mountain." ChavNu said. It wasn't a question.

"I know. SenTot talked often with his warrior leaders of invading the land, but they never did."

"Of course not. GosRati—" She had more to say but lost the words after saying his name.

"GosRati." MadSu said. "He rules from within the mountain and beyond. One clan. Countless warriors. They all bow to him. He's the only one SenTot feared."

"Yet he never came." ChavNu said. "He never left the mountain and likely never will..." She hesitated, debating whether or not to speak her thoughts. Her sister could read her face, however.

"Speak sister."

"The Storm Clans whispered about him. They said he does not leave the mountain because he **can not** leave the mountain. They said he died on the mountain and his spirit is tied to it."

She smirked. "If his spirit was tied to it in death, then who commands the Clan on the other side? Do they follow a specter?"

"I do not know, my sister." ChavNu said, her head shaking at her own foolish-sounding words. Yet she could not stop now; she had said this much and now needed to finish. "I only know GosRati has never been a threat—"

"He is man. They are all threats." MadSu said, speaking with a tone of finality. "No clan led by a man will live as long as I do. This is not about conquest. It is not about killing for sport or thrill. It is not about death at all; this is about life." MadSu allowed herself a moment to look over the sea of warriors around her, many of whom were calmly treating wounds that would have put men into a

THE LADY IN THE LAKE

panic.

"You do not fight for us." ChavNu said, drawing an angry look from her sister. "You do not fight for yourself either. You fight for your son."

"Yes, that's true." she conceded, turning toward a nearby pool where an elder attendant was watching over her son; her last living son…her last child at all.

"Alive or not, you said it yourself:" ChavNu said, reclaiming her sister from her distant thoughts. "GosRati was the only clan-leader to frighten SenTot, and your husband was the most feared on **this** side of the mountain."

"My husband is a fleeting memory." MadSu said, straightening her back. "And when this is over GosRati will be just as forgotten."

*****

MadSu's army marched south and east with the tall peaks of the Dead Mountains creeping ever closer. At night they looked like a hundred hooded specters hovering in the stars. During the day they were grey and white fingers stretching to the heavens. Every hour brought them closer to the mountains, and to the desert on the other side, where the sand snakes had long since been driven into hiding.

She knew the legends of the great snakes and of their defeat at the hands of SenTot's ancestor…or so she'd been told. Though she never doubted his boasting before, she did begin to wonder how much of it was true when other women of her nation spoke similar—but different—stories about the sand snakes and their vanquishing.

"It was the ancestor of my clan-leader Ramata who pulled a streaking light from the sky, fashioned it as whip and drove the sand serpents into the sea." one woman said, while baking cakes on a flat stone. Others gathered around scoffed at her.

"He pulled down the sky?" said one, turning away with a smirk.

"It was a time of great magic!" she insisted. MadSu had meant to walk by without note, but she lingered out of sight to listen.

"There is no magic, Poru." another lady said as the old woman flipped her cake with a sour expression. "If there was we'd use it ourselves."

Another one leaned in, stretched her arm across the circle of debaters. "We'd whisk ourselves to the mountains and crush the last of the men for once and for good." she said, driving a fist into her hand.

"No, we'd whisk away to some other land. Greener and more peaceful—"

"There is no such land." MadSu said, stepping toward them. They all averted their eyes, wary of what she might say. "We have the land we

THE LADY IN THE LAKE

have and there is no magic to assist us." She wasn't angry, but she knew dreaming of far away lands would not win them any battles, and the battle to come would test their full resolve. "We continue onward tomorrow. Eat and rest until then." She walked away, unable to resist her own thoughts of a greener and more peaceful land. Unlike them, however, she knew the land she had was all she'd ever have. It was up to her to bring peace to it.

A few clans met them on the way, but MadSu noticed a curious thing as they journeyed; the clan-leaders were not fighting her or even—as some had tried before—bothering to offer her a bribe to pass quietly (which she never accepted anyway). Instead they were surrendering, aware of the fame of her nation and of their great victory at the Father and Mother Rivers. The men became servants, unarmed and restrained. The feeble and children were cared for in the inner-part of their great roving nation, while the fighting women were trained and added to the warriors who held the perimeter.

By the time they made camp at the foot of the Dead Mountains, their warriors numbered sixty-thousand, and the whole nation over twice as many more. They camped a night and a day with no hint of activity from the mountain.

"When did our scouts enter?" MadSu asked.

"They were several days ahead of us," ChavNu said. "and moving faster. They should have reached the other side by now."

"They should be on their way back if you ask me." Riboora said under a furrowed brow.

"Let's give them another day." MadSu said, turning away and ending the conversation.

It took less than a day for word to finally reach the camp. MadSu was summoned from her tent at dusk by a stunned servant. She grabbed her sword and pushed open her tent as people were transfixed on something ahead of them. She pushed through the crowd to see a lone figure, running from the mountain toward the camp.

"One of ours?" MadSu asked.

"It is ShNar." Riboora said. "One of our scouts."

She was running with a frantic gate, arms flailing. A clump of dirt burst from the ground text to her and she immediately began zigging and zagging as she ran, revealing a pursuer chasing after her.

"GO!" MadSu yelled, as she led her warriors toward the assailant. As they approached she realized the enemy was not running but riding. His horse was gaining on his target and would likely reach her before they would.

There was no use shouting for her scout to turn and fight. No sense in telling her to hurry. She was no match for the beast and its rider, who ran her down, stepped over her limp body and continued charging toward the warriors. The

THE LADY IN THE LAKE

women pulled back and stopped, wondering if the single fighter was stupid enough to throw his life away in a foolhardy charge, outnumbered twenty-thousand to one.

He was.

They cut him down along with his beast, who gave more of a fight than he did. MadSu dealt the killing blow to the animal, then noticed in the distance the scout was still moving, crawling toward them. She ran to help her, turning her over and holding her head in her lap.

The scout's lips were dry and cracked, her hair caked in dirt and sweat. "Get me water!" MadSu cried, turning back to her nation. The scout's hand touched her cheek and turned her face back toward her own. She tried to speak but only a dry, rattled breath left her lips. She pulled MadSu close, pressing her ear against her lips.

"He's waiting for you…" she whispered before sinking, limply, to the ground.

They entered the mountain range that night, despite appeals by ChavNu and Riboora to wait till morning. There was no use in waiting, she decided. He was not coming to her; she would have to go to him. She took thousands of warriors with her, but left thousands more to watch after the rest.

"I assume this is GosRati's plan." Riboora said. "To draw us in and force us to fight with a smaller army."

"We should have taken more." ChavNu agreed. "There are no more enemies on that side of the mountain; our people are safe."

"They are not safe until the land is whole." MadSu said. "And the land will not be whole until it is whole. As long as GosRati lives our nation will never truly rule the land."

"Found something!" a voice called from the front of the assembly. MadSu ran ahead to the exit point of the cave they'd been searching. The sky was still dark but the moon and stars provided enough of a glow to reveal a lone figure standing below them, in the middle of a huge clearing.

He was dressed in black, with a bald head and a beard of white. His dark skin and darker robes almost camouflaged him from their eyes; if it weren't for his almost-glowing beard they likely wouldn't have seen him. "GosRati?" MadSu shouted.

A voice responded, though not with a shout; it fluttered into her ear as though he was standing right beside her. "GosRati is dead." the voice answered.

"And who are you then?" MadSu asked, her voice barely above a whisper.

"I am Merkall, as your people know me. I guard this land."

"Guard it from what?"

"From whom." he corrected her.

THE LADY IN THE LAKE

"You tell me." she insisted.

"From men like GosRati, men who seize too much power and who…disrupt the balance in the land."

"What about his army?"

"Dead too." Merkall answered matter-of-factly. "Not three days ago."

"We should meet." MadSu said and, not waiting for a response, stepped down the rocky slope to the ground below to meet the man face-to-face.

"I'm glad to meet the famous warrior woman of the WuStyni."

"Are you alive or something else?" MadSu asked, wondering about the tales of ghosts in these mountains.

"Oh I'm very much alive."

"We're not calling ourselves that anymore." MadSu said abruptly. "WuStyni. That's the name of the people now dead. We are something new."

"Very well." he said, still holding a faint smile, as though he was privy to an inside joke and wasn't keen to share it. "What do you call your nation?"

"I don't know yet. We'll decide after we're done."

"Aren't you done?" Merkall said, looking around at the emptiness around them. "There are no more men to conquer."

"There are always more men to conquer."

she responded as she drew a blade from her hip and, with great speed, sliced open the man's chest. He stumbled backwards and fell to the ground, gaping at her with a look of shock.

"They will send another..." he sputtered.

"Who?"

"Those who are...above..." He had more to say but he collapsed before he could. MadSu had heard enough anyway.

"Let them send another." she said, taking the man's staff from his cold, dead hand and feeling its magic course through her. "I will kill him too."

THE LADY IN THE LAKE

six-hundred years later...

MATTHEW L. MARTIN

CHAPTER 1: AGAINST PROTOCOL

A white tabard emblazoned with a yellow sun stretched out across a stone slab. Around it was the interior of a partially-lit cave, with dull-blue rocks of unnatural variety forming the uneven floor and jagged walls, against which a pair of highly unusual-looking people stood. A burning altar illuminated half the room, casting streaking black shadows on the wall in front of the man and woman.

He was small, no taller than a child and with a child's body as well. His head was three times what it should have been, however, and was only more striking due to the lightning bolt of blue and

THE LADY IN THE LAKE

red that was painted across his face, and the large tear-drop of black hair that rested on the exact top of his head. From behind he no doubt looked like a child wearing an oversized mask; from the front, the lines of his face and the life in his eyes gave him away.

The librarian's face showed no sign of aging, despite twenty-years that had passed since the wearer of the tabard had died. The blood that had oozed out of Arthur's belly had long-since been washed clean. The tear from the blade that ripped him open and took the life out of him (as far as anyone knew) was still in place; the librarian might have been able to mend it but he saw no reason.

Next to him stood a woman of radiant beauty. Alone, she might've looked like the queen of a far away country, isolated from war or distress. Her expression was grave, her posture stiff; she seemed old by the way she carried herself but her face would have passed for a woman of thirty. Hair of pearl and a dress of shimmering sky-blue, The Lady rested a small hand on the fabric of Arthur's tabard, like a mother holding the hand of a child while he slept.

The two of them stood quietly next to the slab in the cave, neither one speaking or seeming to have even a reason too. Whatever conversations they'd had were over; now they were content to wait quietly. After a long stretch of silence, the thing they were waiting for finally happened. Footsteps shuffled on the rocky floor behind them but neither turned to see the approaching man. He stepped into the room, tall and muscular, draped in shades of lilac with a six-winged dragon painted on the front of his garb.

"The mouth is closed, but I can't say how long I can keep it that way." the man in lilac answered.

"Thank you Seraph, it'll be long enough." The Lady responded, still staring at Arthur's tabard, seeing through it and imagining a man filling it.

"Just because I did this doesn't mean I approve." Seraph said flatly. He'd said variations of the same thing several times already but no matter how many times he told her, he felt he needed to say it again…and no matter how many times he told her, she refused to budge.

"Thank you again Seraph." she answered without a hint of impatience. She knew his concerns and though she was choosing to ignore them she did not wish to slight him with a lecture of her own. This was not his fight. He was not a guardian the way she was; he had only one job, to protect the entrance to the sacred relic. *I have much bigger challenges to deal with*, she knew.

"You promised us a vote." the Librarian said abruptly.

The Lady looked at him with surprise; she

THE LADY IN THE LAKE

hadn't been expecting that sort of talk. "I wasn't aware you disagreed with my idea."

"I never committed to it one way or another. Truth be told I always thought you'd come to your senses."

"Clearly I have not." she answered as she scooped up the white cloth and rearranged it so that it was facing her; The Lady's eyes fell on the sun crest in the middle of the fabric. A heavy sigh rolled out of her. "I don't expect either of you to understand or agree. But as I say, I thank you both for your help." Neither man responded, not even with a polite nod. The Lady noticed and spun around to face them both. "Alright then. Let's clear the air before we do this, hm?"

As if they'd just been waiting for permission, both men lurched forward, ready to spill out their plurality of arguments against The Lady's ideas. "It's unethical!" the Librarian said.

"It's against protocol!" Seraph added.

The Lady scoffed. "Protocol…you know what protocol is in this situation?"

"There **isn't** protocol for this situation!" the Librarian answered.

"There is; it's the same protocol for everything else we do down here…which is to say, we're supposed to just make it up as we go along." There was a twinge of bitterness to her voice that was undeniable.

"Please." the Librarian snorted. "If they

wanted to do this they'd have done it themselves."

"You please!" The Lady retorted. "When have they ever been so active with what goes on down here?"

"They send guardians down all the time." Seraph countered. "Whenever a guardian dies, loses a Kingdom or retires…they send. They're active."

"That's not the same as this." The Lady said, holding a hand over Arthur's empty shirt. "They send guardians, yes, like a factory churning out products. All with the same commandment: Keep the balance. That's it."

"Yes that's it." The Librarian was looking at her now with great worry. "This is far more radical than I thought when I agreed to help you. You say there's a great threat growing—"

"I have seen it." she insisted.

"Fine. So I helped. I brought you the body and the sword. Seraph helped: We're at his gateway. We've done our part Lady, don't ask us to do any more."

"The body and the gateway are worthless if you don't agree to do this." She willed her tense and impatient face to relax. "I can't do it alone. We need a majority."

"I'm sorry…" the Librarian turned away from her piercing gaze. "I thought I could give you what you wanted and go back to the Tree in peace, but…I can't let you do this. It's not right. Seraph's

THE LADY IN THE LAKE

right, it's against everything—"

"I'll do it." Serpah's voice interrupted him. He stepped forward beside the stone slab. His eyes were down, his expression defeated. He didn't want to do this, but he was willing to trust The Lady who'd never steered him wrong before. She was right to say they'd all been on earth with very little guidance from above. They were basically on their own and she being the oldest had always been the wise counsel they needed from time to time. He couldn't turn on her now.

"Excellent." she said flatly. "That's two out of three. That's a majority." She turned to the Librarian who seemed frozen by Seraph's decision. "Your conscience can remain clear and you can return to the Library."

"If it's all the same I'd like to stay…I won't interfere."

"Of course." she said smiling as the tiny man shuffled away from the stone slab and from the burning altar nearby. "I will handle the altar." she said to Seraph. "You open the gateway."

"Just tell me when."

"Now, please." she said immediately. Seraph raised an open hand toward the wall opposite him. A flood of golden light filled the room as a doorway appeared where there had not been one before. The fire in the altar flickered, with bursts of embers bursting in all directions. A long shape slid from the top of that altar, gliding on air, controlled by The Lady. It rested on the slab next to her, burning the fabric of the tabard underneath. "I'll be back shortly." she said casually as she stepped into the golden light and disappeared.

*****

"None of this makes any sense." Arthur raised his eyes—bleary from lack of sleep—away from the brittle pages of yet another tome he was pouring over. "This one says six days, but this one..." He leaned over to another book he'd discarded hours earlier "says six eons...What even is an eon?"

"It's kind of a catch-all word for 'really long time.'" The man hovering over him said. Like Arthur, he too was garbed in robes of white trimmed with gold. Unlike Arthur, he seemed perfectly content with the environment around them.

How long Arthur had been...wherever he was, he didn't know. His mind was not a fog; he perfectly remembered every moment of his life (as best as one could), right up to the moment when he was spun around and sliced by Templar Knight. The next thing he remembered was waking up in the upper room and seeing...

Nope, nopenopenope, he told himself as his mind began to wander. *Focus.* He turned back to the book in front of him, decorated with illustrations depicting planets and stars and lots

THE LADY IN THE LAKE

and lots of words haphazardly written around the drawings. *I don't even speak Hebrew, how am I able to read this?* he asked himself, and not for the first time. He could recall sessions with other white-dressed men where many languages were taught to him. He'd sat through enough classes to fill ten years of learning, yet it felt like he'd only arrived yesterday.

"You're day-dreaming again." the man hovering over him said, snapping Arthur out of his haze.

"Is it day-dreaming or night-dreaming or what? There's never a sunrise or sunset in this place."

"Are you tired, Arthur?"

"No."

"Then what does it matter?"

"I'm not tired, just curious. I saw Gwen…yesterday? No…" He had to think for a moment. He definitely saw her, but it couldn't have been yesterday. So much had happened since then…On the other hand it **felt** like only yesterday.

"You're going to drive yourself crazy doing that, you know." the man said, smirking at Arthur's furrowed brow, deep in contemplation. "Your wife came here by means of a vision. You came here…by some other method."

"Always with your secrets, Corvis."

"Would you believe that I really don't know

much more than you do? No one tells me anything around here either; I've just learned to roll with it and not get so distraught trying to figure it out.."

"Well that's you but it's not me." Arthur looked up from his book to consider the face of the man who'd been with him every step of the way inside this place...whatever it was. "How long have **you** been here?"

Corvis only grinned at him. "Long enough to know better than to expect an answer to that question." Arthur continued staring, however, clearly expecting a more concrete answer. "Look, there is no **how long** in a place like this."

"Certainly feels like there is."

"That's only because you're still thinking about the world you left behind. You've got work to do here and now. There's no time to dwell on the former."

"Yeah, well I don't even know—"

"Arthur!" a voice shouted to him from the room below them.

"Just a minute!" he shouted back, not even pausing to consider how unusual it was to be shouted at from below; it had never happened before. "I've been up here reading these books—"

"Arthur!"

"—and half of them are contradictory, and I know you say that's because people tell the same story in different ways, but I don't even know what the story is and no one—"

THE LADY IN THE LAKE

"Arthur please!"

"Just a minute, I'm right in the middle of a rant! No one has even told me what the point of reading these books is. You told me I was preparing for something but I don't even know—"

"Arth—" The voice stopped abruptly as a few other men and women—seated around the table with books just as Arthur was—suddenly leapt to their feet and hurried for the doorway. A figure dressed not like the others had climbed the stairs and was trying to force her way into their room.

"Do I know you?" Arthur asked. She was radiant, almost glowing with beauty. Her platinum hair was pulled back into a bun and her blue outfit seemed to float as if she was underwater.

"Vivianne." Corvis stepped in between them. He gestured to the others who were holding her at bay and quickly they released their grip. "Why have you come here?"

"I'm come for the King."

"You've come to the wrong place...and time."

"No, not that King." She craned her neck over his shoulder to lock eyes with Arthur once more.

"Let's have a minute." Corvis said, looking around the room to the confused faces. Most of them got the hint and dispersed down the stairs but a few lingered, staring warily at The Lady in blue. "It's alright." the man nodded, shooing them away. "She used to go to this school."

"A long time ago." The Lady answered.

"Yes and you did not stay. You should have; you'd have been a great teacher."

"They needed me below."

"You're remarkable enough to be needed anywhere you go. But...here nor there. Why have you come?"

She did not continue with Corvis but instead side-stepped him to face Arthur. "To answer your question, no, you do not know me. But I know you. I've been watching over your family for generations now. I—"

"Wait...I **do** know you. I saw you in Merlin's vision. He pushed me in the water and you scooped me up."

"That was your ancestor but yes, I remember that well."

"You've been watching me all this time."

"All of you, yes. From a far, though I've let many things go by without intervention."

"I'd say so. Murder and plotting have followed me around for years, not to mention headless giants...and you've been sitting back doing nothing?"

"I don't expect you to understand all that I do, or why I sometimes do **not** do, but—"

"He ought to understand, he's training right now." Corvis piped in.

THE LADY IN THE LAKE

"That will have to be postponed." she said, much to Corvis' disbelief. "You are needed back."

"Back where?" Arthur asked. It was a stupid question but he was feeling overwhelmed by the moment, and when that happens, a stupid question or two is bound to slip out.

"Below. You've been gone a long time. I could take you back to the moment…" She trailed off at the sight of Corvis expression turning fierce. "No." she said, correcting herself. "I can take you through the gateway to the time I left behind."

"What time is that?"

"Just before the storm hits the old lands. Twenty years after your death if you must know."

"Twen—no, I can't go back twenty years later. I want to go back to the library. If you can take me back then take me back to that moment."

"No Arthur." Corvis said softly but he was being ignored.

"If I must go back then let me live out the days I've lost. We would have more time to prepare for whatever's coming."

"Enough. Say your peace Vivianne and then go. Arthur is not leaving but if have a message to deliver then get on with it. His time is not yet come."

"I know it isn't Corvis." The Lady said as she frowned and looked to the floor. "But his time will have to come early."

"It is too soon."

"You sent Mera! She was too soon and yet you sent her!"

"I did not send Mera. I was overruled, and since I've had no word to send Arthur I will not allow—"

"What are you sending me into?" Arthur said, joining the conversation he was at the center of.

"The war I've been trying to resist for generations. Morgana's final push to control your world."

"Not your place." Corvis said. He might've been saying a lot more in his head but those were the words that both Arthur and The Lady heard. "Your job is not to lead armies against armies or resist plots or whatever task you've given yourself. Your job is to keep the scales level, to give men the freedom to choose good, **not** to fight on their side."

The Lady swelled up with anger. "This is not some ruler of men rising to kill and conquer. This is not about letting men choose and preserving the balance. This is one of us. Morgana has taken the first move against the earth! I only want to stop her."

"Balance—" Corvis began but was cut off.

"This **is** balance! She must be stopped."

"I agree." Arthur said. He understood, at best, half of what they were talking about, but he knew enough to know Morgana must be defeated.

"Return to your books." Corvis told him

THE LADY IN THE LAKE

bluntly. "You do not understand this issue."

"What does that even mean?!" Now it was Arthur's turn to resist Corvis. "Ever since I've been here you people have jerked me around and I've gone along with it because goodness knows I have no idea what I'm doing otherwise. But you're not going to stand there and tell me I don't have a choice to go back to—"

Faster than a blink and without even a hint that anything had changed, Arthur found himself in total darkness. "Sit." Corvis' voice echoed around him, distant yet ever-present.

"Not the void!" Arthur shouted to no response. He'd been here once before. It was his time-out place, the place they stuck him when he became too unruly and insistent on asking questions. But almost as soon as he arrived, a tear in the darkness appeared, shimmering blue and white. Through it stepped The Lady, accompanied by Corvis.

"—cannot know, it would destroy him." Corvis was saying as they stepped through.

"We're going." The Lady said.

"Good, I'm ready." Arthur replied, spinning around to see the two of them still facing each other.

"We're not done debating this." Corvis replied.

"We've debated this for eighty years now. There's nothing more to say." she replied.

Arthur stupidly looked around as though he should have been able to perceive such a vast passage of time. Of course he couldn't; time had never worked the way it was supposed to since he came there.

"There can be no discussion of the future," Corvis said, raising a finger toward The Lady, "or of the causality."

"What...causality?" Arthur asked but was not surprised to have this question ignored.

"He will only know what he needs to." The Lady said, smiling at her victory.

"You are meddling with very strict rules here Vivianne. I am not responsible for what happens when you take him. If he dies, the future—"

"Worry about your school," The Lady said lowering Corvis' stern finger with her gentle hand, "I'll worry about time. It always tells."

"You're talking about me still, right? You can see me?"

"Are you ready?" she said to Arthur, finally looking at him.

"I was born ready." Arthur said without thinking.

"Of that, Arthur..." The Lady began but before she could finish, the slit of light in the dark room expanded and enveloped them. Just as quickly the light faded and turned blue and orange while the air chilled around him. He was lying on

THE LADY IN THE LAKE

a slab of rock, looking at a trio of people, all of whom he'd seen before: The Seraph-Knight he fought to enter the gateway to the Library, the Librarian he met before the Templar and Sir Morian crashed the party, and The Lady who'd come to collect him. His eyes fell on her as she finished her previous statement: "...I have no doubt."

MATTHEW L. MARTIN
CHAPTER 2 : RABBLE

Raph's tavern sat nestled inside a narrow crook along the south side of the River Loire, about half a day's ride to Orleans. The quiet and unassuming man who inherited the establishment was always good to offer cheap prices but at the offset cost of never asking him any questions about his past, how he came to own the bar, who the previous owner was, or anything that he considered "prying" and "not drinking talk."

Though mild mannered, the slender and straight-faced Raph knew a bar was only as good as its reputation, thus he hoped for a bar fight at least once a week ("but no more!"), if only to keep

THE LADY IN THE LAKE

his establishment being talked about as travellers made their way to and from Orleans.

Walking amongst the tables, eavesdroppers could hear all manner of chit-chat, gossip, conspiracy theories and even revolution-plotting. In one corner, a trio of gruff-looking ex-soldiers were complaining about the state of France under Queen Arabella, griping about her majesty's high taxes and rumors of war with the Southern Celts of Iberia.

It was nearly twenty years ago that France and Rome officially ended their on-again, off-again war, culminating in the relinquishing of the lands in southwest France to the Roman Empire. Not ten years later, the Southern Celts decided to poke the bear and invade Rome's reclaimed land; the two sides have been locked in a war of attrition ever since, with Arabella claiming neutrality while secretly (though it was an open secret) aiding Rome and the Emperor-Pope who recently ascended to the throne.

At another table, a pair of drunkards debated (loudly) the rumors of an eastern Kingdom sweeping across the desert cities beyond the Holy Lands. No one had seen or heard any definitive proof that such an invading force existed, but enough people had commented on "death sweeping across the east" for the rumors to be passed off as idle talk. Something was happening over there but no one yet knew what.

MATTHEW L. MARTIN

Tucked away in the bar's darkest corner, under an extinguished light, sat a quartet of misfits, doing their best not to attract attention to themselves. "Should be soon." Petro said to the rest of the group. His squinted eyes projected great wisdom and his soft, raspy voice often forced you to listen carefully to hear his every word. Passers-by would often do a double-take as they noticed him; a man in the middle of France, who dressed like the oriental traders that peddle jewelry in the big cities (not to mention his thin mustache and hair pulled back into a top-knot) was not often seen with his sort of company.

"He might've gotten arrested. There was a Constable in Dijon that seemed to recognize him. He might've followed us." Jay said warily, bouncing one knee up and down in a blur of nervous energy. He was every bit Petro's opposite. Where Petro was older and calm no matter what, Jay was barely eighteen, a mess of twisted red curls and matching freckles, and a worry over every shadow that moved across his vision.

"Just relax and wait. If something happened we'll handle it. We're getting our money either way." Marcella said firmly.

"How will we handle it? If the Constable—"

"How do we always handle it, Jay? They throw us in jail, we break out. Pretend it's a game; now sit still." Marcella put her hand on Jay's leg, forcing it still for the first time since they sat down.

THE LADY IN THE LAKE

She was thirty-five and looked as gorgeous as the day Eric met her, ten years earlier. Sharp as a tack and quick on her feet, there was no one better to manage the business of their business.

"This is not a game, Marcella." Petro turned his eyes slowly toward her. "If the boy speaks true and the Constable is following—"

"First of all, it's just us here Petro; drop the accent." Marcella held her gaze until Petro's shoulders drooped a bit in defeat. "Second, there is no Constable." She turned back to Jay, who was now bobbing his other leg up and down. "What you saw was a traffic guard, writing a ticket to a horse that was illegally parked."

"It could've been Eric's horse." Jay said, wide-eyed. "Tell her Petro."

"His worry is not unfounded." Petro said, still only barely whispering.

"Petro." Marcella said with eyes that weren't in the mood for games.

The Asian(?) man frowned and slumped back in his chair. "Alright fine." he said a little more loudly, suddenly finding a French accent. "The kid just wants his money, why you bustin' his balls?"

"It's not the money, I'm worried about Eric!" Jay insisted.

"You let me worry about Eric." Marcella said before turning to the remaining two figures at the table. "Don't you have anything to contribute?" she asked the large man opposite her.

"I think Dun has to pee." Fortigo said plainly. He grinned stupidly, stretching his overweight face behind his messy straw-colored hair and matching beard. A small man was sitting next to him, with the most vicious expression on his face. When Fortigo scooped him up, Dun flashed a supremely murderous glare at him, but his arms and legs remained limp while the gentle giant slung him into a makeshift pack on his back. "He gets moody when he doesn't go regularly. I'll be back; don't leave without me!" The rest of the table watched him clumsily stroll away, oblivious to the look of loathing the helpless Dun was giving him from behind.

Not thirty seconds after Fortigo disappeared, the front doors of the tavern creaked open and Eric stepped in, face lined and hair grey. A satchel he wasn't carrying when he separated from the group was dangling from his belt and a look of supreme annoyance was all over his expression. "They wanted to haggle about the price." he said as he sat down in Dun's vacant seat.

"We thought the Constable got you." Jay said with all seriousness.

"Who?" Eric asked, looking weary and waving for a drink to be brought over.

"No we didn't." Marcella said. "Any trouble?"

"Other than them wanting to pay fifty

THE LADY IN THE LAKE

instead of the agreed-to sixty-five? No." He dropped the satchel on the table with a clunk and let the flap fall over, revealing an assortment of gold coins.

"How much is in there?" Petro asked, completely dropping any pretense of being a stoic old man from the far East.

"A hundred." Eric answered gruffly as he snatched the mug from the waiter's hand and downed the contents in one gulp.

"How'd you pull that off?!" Jay asked in awe.

"I told you they wanted to haggle. We haggled."

Whatever questions the rest of the table had were cut short by the sound of a raucous fight happening on the other side of the room. "It's only Monday; too early for a bar fight." Marcella said. One patron went flying across the room as two more dove onto the large target they were fighting. A bag went sliding across the wooden floor, sending patrons scooting away from it with looks of terror on their faces.

"Dun!" Jay shouted, pointing to the bag. The rest of the table found him with their eyes soon after; the tiny man was still wrapped tight in the pack, snapping like a caged animal and jerking his head side to side. "Where's Fortigo?"

"I'm guessing he's on the bottom of that pile." Eric said, rising slowly from the table like the fifty-year-old he was. Marcella joined him, hip-daggers already drawn. Petro continued eating his fried pickles, content to let the younger brawlers have their fun. "That's enough!" Eric shouted.

A few of the fighters paused to see him standing there, looking about as intimidating as a half-century old man could (which is to say, not very), before resuming their pummeling of the near-giant. Fortigo had his hands over his head to absorb the blows, but though he could have easily overpowered the lot of them he did nothing but take the abuse. "I said—" Eric started to repeat his words but the quick action of Marcella stopped him. She had two men flipped over the nearest table and a third on the floor with a knife to his throat before another could raise a fist against her.

"Raph, what is this stuff?" Marcella asked, sniffing the fresh stains on her downed-opponent's shirt. "It smells fantastic."

"It's uh..." a voice emerged from under the bar and soon after a thin man rose holding a dusty bottle close to his face. "Grape and honey wine. Came from storage."

"Thanks Marcella." Fortigo said as he slowly pulled himself up. Other than a bruise under his right eye he seemed unscathed.

"You okay?" she said, pointing to the purple streak above his cheek.

"Oh yeah, Dun did that. Poor thing accidentally head-butted me." He looked over her

THE LADY IN THE LAKE

shoulder to the pack that Jay was warily holding. Dun was shooting him a look of pure loathing. "Turns out he didn't need to pee after all. It was...the other."

"I got it." Marcella said, stopping him from elaborating.

Fortigo lumbered to Jay to collect his strapped-in companion and slung him back over his shoulder. Dun almost took a bite out of Fortigo's ear but missed him by an inch; the gentle giant seemed entirely unaware of the near miss. "Thanks Jay." he said to the young man, rubbing his messy red hair a little too vigorously, causing strands of scarlet to fly into the air.

"I think we've overstayed our welcome." Eric said, signaling for his group to exit. Marcella was first one out the door but she did a 180 and returned to the bar as soon as her feet stepped outside.

"Let's go out the back." she said.

"There is no back, unless you want to swim." Eric said, frowning at her. "What's out there?"

"Nothing, I just...let's stay and drink more."

"But you don't drink. You just like the smell." Eric side-stepped her and pushed the door open despite her pulling him back. The late-afternoon sun cast an orange glow over the road. Everything looked just as it did when Eric had last left it, with an assortment of horses tied up in the stables to their right, next to Raph's storage building. Across from them were the rent-houses for the bums too drunk to ride home. Other than a carriage resting by a rent-house, secured to a pair of brown horses, nothing was— "Wait…" Eric said, examining the carriage more carefully. "Is that…"

"Eric!" Raph's voice pierced through the post-brawl chatter and jolted him away from the door. He rarely raised his voice but when he did his regular customers knew to listen carefully. "That's the last time you and your…friends start a Monday fight in my establishment!"

"Here." Eric said, flipping him one of the gold coins from his satchel. "Sorry."

"Sorry's not good enough. One fight a week, that's the goal. More than that and we become **that** bar. I don't want to become one of **those** bars, attracting **those** sort of customers. One a week, that's it. And now I have to keep the peace until Sunday!"

"Alright, here…" Eric handed him two more gold coins, which caused a collective back-stiffening from the rest of the party that lingered near the door.

"You're paying him out of your share, right?" Jay asked.

Before Eric could respond with what almost certainly would have been a condescending retort, the door behind him opened and a parade of

THE LADY IN THE LAKE

people pushed their way past, with more than a few of them bumping into his shoulder, paying him no mind. Each of them was dressed with matching white tabards, adorned by a rounded red cross. Their clothes were baggy, with no mail underneath; these were soldiers off duty, just passing through.

"We need a table for ten and two rent houses." the lead man said to Raph, who nodded and scurried away to push two tables together.

"I knew it." Eric said, nostrils flaring with fast-rising rage. "Templar."

"What do we do?" Jay said, eyes moving from the collection of white-Knights and his own party.

"Nothing." Marcella answered before Eric could say something rash. "We go sit back down over there, far away from them."

"Shouldn't we just leave?" Petro asked, whispering but not in his faux-Asian accent.

"No, there are more outside."

Eric took that as an invitation and muscled his way past the group to get another look outside. Sure enough, another five Templar were unloading bags from their cross-emblazoned carriage to one of the rent houses, being overseen by a sneering man dressed head to toe in blood-red. "Oh!" Eric snarled. More words would have followed, likely laced with profanity, but Fortigo's giant hands were quick to press against his back and help him away from the doors back to their table.

Raph already had a stiff drink waiting for him when he sat down. Eric downed it at once and slammed the empty mug on the table, nearly shattering it.

"Feel better?" Marcella asked him.

"We have to kill them." Eric responded icily.

"Do we? We **have** to? Who's paying us to do that?"

"No one's paying us to kill anybody." Jay said, a hint of panic in his young voice. "I'm just paid to sneak and unlock windows and occasionally pose as someone's kid."

"I'm not killing anyone that didn't kill me first." Fortigo said, trying to sound serious. "And Dun wouldn't hurt a fly." he added, not even looking down at his tiny companion, whose lip was curled in his general direction.

"You promised me you were done with this." Marcella said. "You said you'd killed your last one ten years ago."

"That was before they started roaming the French countryside!" Eric was whispering but his gestures were intense enough to attract attention from more than a few drunkards nearby. The Templar seemed entirely unaware that they were the subject of such an intense conversation, however.

"What do you want to do? You want to tell

THE LADY IN THE LAKE

the Queen who she can make deals with? Rome has a right of travel agreement with France. They have every legal right to be here."

Eric looked at her like she'd killed his best friend. "First of all, those are not Roman soldiers. Those are hired thugs."

"So are we, mate." Petro said, shrugging.

Eric ignored that. "And second, they have no business being this far from the southern border."

"They're probably headed to Orleans." Jay said, foolishly interjecting himself into the conversation. "It's a major city in the area."

"Do we have a travel agreement or a commerce agreement?" Eric snapped at him. Jay of course had no answer, not even knowing enough about the politics or the meanings of those phrases to argue. He just wanted to be part of the group, poor kid.

"Just...let it be." Marcella said calmly. "We'll let them drink and talk and when they all go to the rent house we'll leave."

"Why don't we just leave now?" Petro asked.

"Because Eric has a pretty big warrant on his head." Marcella replied. "The last thing we need is to be seen hurrying away as soon as a bunch of Templar show up. They're likely to follow."

"Let them follow." Eric said coolly. Marcella only sighed but it was a mixture of sadness over her lover's persistent bitterness and relief that he seemed resigned to her plan. A few minutes of silence and a few more rounds followed.

A figure approached the table, dressed in a leather jerkin and a hood that concealed a pair of shifty eyes. "Excuse me." he said, not sounding very apologetic.

"No thanks." Eric replied without looking at him, taking him for a waiter.

"Eric." Marcella said. Unlike the others, she spotted him the moment he walked into the bar and tracked his movements as he meandered his way over to them. Eric looked up to meet the stare of the stranger.

"I have somewhat of an offer for you and your… companions." the man said, examining the table of assorted ruffians.

"We're not doing business. We're just drinking." Eric replied, holding up his empty mug before turning back to the bar to signal for a refill. A moment of silence lingered between them until the waiter came with another mug of mead.

"This one is on me." the man said, handing the waiter a gold coin and flashed the table a slight grin. He waiter hurried himself away and shoved the coin in his pocket as quickly as he could.

Eric smiled back at the stranger, albeit his was a bit more mocking. "Where are you from?" he asked.

"I am from…around."

THE LADY IN THE LAKE

Marcella leaned in with a smile that mimicked Eric's. "Yeah, see if you were from around here, you'd know Raph doesn't let his waiters handle the tab. You wanna buy my drink you gotta pay the man directly. But you made that kid's day, at least."

"Does your companion speak for you?" the man said, still looking at Eric.

"Oh you're not going to want to ignore her like that." Eric said, darting his eyes back and forth between the stranger and Marcella. She was casually resting a hand on the handle of a dagger strapped to her thigh. The man shifted in his stance and cleared his throat slightly.

"Perhaps we should start over."

"That might be wise." Marcella said, removing her hand from the blade.

"I am O'Mare. I represent a man called Graves. He—"

"Take me to him." Eric said flatly.

"I'm sorry?"

"I don't do business without knowing who I'm doing business with."

"I thought you said you weren't doing business. Just drinking."

Petro leaned forward to make his presence known, and spoke with his put-on far-eastern accent: "Clearly you know who we are. You know what we do. You wish to procure our services. But we are a cautious bunch."

"Yeah. Cautious." Jay said, sloshing a bit of his drink while trying to sound intimidating.

"You have quite the assortment or rabble at your disposal, sir." O'Mare's eyes never left Eric's, even as the latter looked around the table while his companions spoke. "My master knows of your exploits. You are apparently the best bunch of mercenaries this side of the Vosporos."

"We are actually a delivery service." Eric said without hesitation. "We ship goods and merchandise from one place to another at a minimal charge."

"We only ever deliver the highest quality of delivery." Marcella added.

"Yes of course." O'Mare nodded. "Well my master thinks you are just the sort he needs." He reached out a hand containing a small, rolled up parchment. Eric did not move to take it.

"I told you," Eric said, "I only do business with faces, not messages."

"Well...He is a private man but I think you'll find his offer generous enough to compensate for your personal scruples."

When Eric still did not budge, Marcella snatched the parchment and broke the seal. "Is this serious?" she asked, looking over the note. Her wide-eyed expression caused Jay and Petro to lean over to get a look at the writing. Fortigo awkwardly tried to lean in as well, but his massive belly only scooted the table forward as he leaned.

THE LADY IN THE LAKE

"We'll want half of this up front." she added.

"I thought you'd say something like that." O'Mare said, smiling as he pulled out a sack and placed it on the table. All the information is there."

"This...is not half." Petro said

"Of course it isn't my foreign friend. That's half of half. Consider that an act of kindness. You'll get the rest of the half if you agree to the assignment. As I say, all the information is in the parchment. Be at Grenoble on the date instructed. Don't miss it; this is a time-sensitive job."

"Anything else?" Marcella asked, having now completely taken over the discussions with Eric sitting and stewing silently next to her.

"Bring whatever weapons you have. There will be danger."

"Oh don't worry there." Fortigo said boldly. "We have mag—" He stopped as Marcella's bug-eyed look shut him up suddenly.

"Very good. Until then." O'Mare said with a nod. He extended a hand toward Eric who did not shake it, but Marcella did and he exited soon after.

"Don't you even want to know how much they're going to pay us for this job?" she asked Eric.

"No." he said, pouting. "I'm not going."

"We're going." she said with finality. "This is the big one. Everyone talks about the big one, well this is our big one. We get this and we can retire to some island on the Great Sea and live happily ever after."

"Sounds wonderful." Jay said, smiling stupidly. Marcella ignored him.

"You go. I don't trust him."

"Oh shut up, that's a stupid thing to say and you know it. We've done lots of jobs for people hiding in the shadows. We're hired thieves, thugs, ruffians; you expect our clientele to be priests and clergymen?

"I didn't get into this to be crook."

"No you got into it to kill Templar to and from jobs."

"Geez Marcella, keep it down!" Jay whispered.

She ignored him (she did that a lot) and pressed on. "Then you met me. And now you want to us to go alone, without you? No, because you promised there would be no going alone any more. You promised that—"

"I know what I promised!" Eric shouted, turning the bar's attention their way.

"Do you just not want to be done? Is that it? Do you not want to retire to peace and happiness? You think you don't deserve that; is that it?"

"Get out of my head."

"Excuse me madam." A voice behind them interrupted their bickering. A Templar was hovering over Eric, looking down at Marcella with a concerned expression. From his fresh face and short hair he looked no older than twenty. "I heard

THE LADY IN THE LAKE

raised voices." he said. "This man might have had a few too many. Is he bothering you?"

"Oh...no." Petro mumbled in his natural accent.

"I was asking the lady, friend." he said, examining Petro's very exotic hairstyle and how it clashed with his very local accent. "Where are you from anyw—" Eric's dagger was in his chest and he was on the floor before he knew what happened.

"No no no no no!" Raph screamed from behind the bar, but it was too late. Chairs were sliding back and Templar were rushing over.

"Yes." Eric said with a deep and satisfying inhale. It'd been far too long since he'd killed a Templar Knight, and he was going to enjoy slipping back into old habits before he took this big job...his last big job. He had nothing else to live for: His friends were dead, his King was dead; all he had was vengeance.

And vengeance was sweeter than wine.

MATTHEW L. MARTIN
CHAPTER 3 : THE ILL-MADE KING

Nine men surrounded him, teeth exposed like carnivorous predators, ready to pounce, to feast and to lick his bones clean when finished with him. Words were said—were being said—but he wasn't listening. His eyes lazily moved from person to person, wondering if they were even listening to themselves. *Likely not*, Mordred thought to himself. *If they were they'd surely have adjourned the meeting and taken a dive off the tallest tower in Cameolot; that's what I'd rather be doing that listening to this.*

A chorus of laughter erupted around him; someone had told another stupid joke. *That would*

THE LADY IN THE LAKE

explain why all their teeth were showing. I suppose they expect me to laugh with them. He flashed an empty, soulless smile, enough to placate them as they all sighed and returned to their menial debates.

"How much longer until I can leave?" Mordred said aloud. *Oh merde, I meant to think that...* He looked around the table with a little more urgency, aware of the look of disdain that had crept over the faces of his advisors...but unsure exactly what it meant. "I was supposed to think that, not say it." he said. The roundtable of men merely smiled pathetically at him, cleared their throats and continued with their discussions.

Mordred had been King of England for nineteen years, though he'd only taken the chair five years ago. *A baby is no good as a ruler, but apparently an overly-sheltered fourteen year old is capable of leading a country?* He thought bitterly about his upbringing; that was commonplace, a regular occurrence that often kissed him goodnight each evening and stirred him awake each morning. It was only recently that he started thinking bitterly about the circumstances of his becoming King.

For the first ten years of his life he might as well have been plucked from the clouds; no one ever told him where he came from, who his father was, why he lived in a giant Castle, and why everyone seemed to treat him differently whenever he'd take trips to various towns and cities in the country. It wasn't until his tenth birthday that his mother finally sat him down to tell him the truth. Her words seared into his mind but it was what came after that made him know how different he really was.

"Your father was the great King Arthur." Gwen had told him. "He died in the middle of a noble quest trying to make the world a better place." She paused after telling him, wondering what questions he might have; if he would want to know more about his father or if he'd want to know more about the day he'd become the King himself. He said nothing, however, so his mother pressed him. "I know you're sad—" she began, but the boy Mordred was quick to interrupt.

"Sad about what?"

"About your father."

"No. I never knew him..."

"Right. Well he was killed by some bad people and that might make you want to grow up looking for revenge. But I want you to know—"

"No."

"No?"

"I don't know what that means." he said to her; it would not be last time he had to ask for help understanding why people feel the way they feel.

"I just don't want you to grow up thinking...look, you're going to be a King one day. Right now the Roundtable is running the country but when you're old enough you'll be making

THE LADY IN THE LAKE

those decisions. Your father and I wouldn't want you trying to hurt the people who killed him."

"Who killed him?"

"Well it was people from Rome. We think they were looking for the same thing your father was. We're not entirely sure. Everyone who went with him was killed." She waited, expecting—perhaps even hoping—for more questions, more interest, more anything. Instead he remained stone-faced. "Are you sad?" Gwen asked him clumsily.

"Am I supposed to be?" Mordred asked in all seriousness.

"Yes.."

"Then I am." he answered, and did his best to recreate the way people look when they are sad. He'd seen those faces before but never understood them. Now he was learning that he would need to at least imitate them if he was to be a good King.

A voice interrupted Mordred's daydreaming, high and condescending, the voice of Sir "Is his grace still with us or should we send a rook to fetch him wherever his mind has led him?" Sir Terance sneered and looked around the table to soak in the mutual sneerings of his companions.

"My apologies Sir Terance, I was just thinking about something I might add to the conversation." Mordred smiled the same empty smile he smiled when he knew he was supposed to smile.

MATTHEW L. MARTIN

When they laugh or when they mock, when they belittle and disrespect, just smile and laugh; play the fool.

"I'm sure his grace has much to offer our discussions on the unrest that has consumed the northern country." Sir Hanbury added with a mocking smile. "What is the King's great suggestion?"

"Enough of this nonsense." Sir White snapped. "Rebels have taken Edinburgh and if we do not act, they will sack York."

"We're a long way from losing York, Sir White, worry not." Sir George said with a put-out expression.

"I wish I had your confidence." Sir Richard said, face grave and tone flat. He was the only one ever to show deference to Mordred, and the only one to resist joining in with the too-relaxed atmosphere that often permeated the weekly Roundtable meetings.

"I wish it too, you could use a little confidence." Sir White retorted. It was the kind of out-of-bounds thumb to an eye that a King—at the head of the roundtable—should have addressed, but Mordred did not stir. Despite the loyalty Sir Richard showed him, the King was never sure when someone had crossed the line between teasing and gross disrespect. Often the line was crossed against him and he had no way of knowing. Thus he would simply smile and

THE LADY IN THE LAKE

chuckle, unsure if he was laughing at himself or playing along with a harmless barb.

His mother tried her best to teach him the difference but as a child the children of the Knights who guarded Camelot would tease him because they knew he would never tell and they would never get in trouble for mocking the future-King. They faces always looked happy so Mordred merely imitated their expressions (it was all he knew to do), oblivious to know if they were mocking or playing.

He snapped out of his daydream to see Sirs Richard and White rolling on the floor, fighting like children. As for the rest of the Roundtable, half were leaning over and shouting like sports spectators, the other half were slumped in their chairs, as desperate as Mordred was for the meeting to end. This wasn't even an unusual meeting; this was just a regular Tuesday.

"Alright." Mordred called out half-heartedly. "Alright!" he tried again. Richard peeled himself away from White—whom he had pinned to the floor—and leapt to his feet at the word of his King. "Is there any new business?"

"Hardly." Sir Grummore said, leaning forward in his chair with a surprised expression. "We have a crisis in the north and you want to talk new business?"

"I didn't actually expect there to be any new business; I just thought you'd all say no and I would adjourn the meeting."

"Adj—your grace, we are on the brink of Civil War!" Grummore was apoplectic. "We need a strategy for how to deal with the rebels in the Scottish territory!"

"We should parlay." Sir Maris said, not waiting for the King to reply.

"Parlay? With traitors?!" Grummore said, looking to Richard for support. They were the foremost military experts on the roundtable and the quickest to call for war.

"No, with the Irish." Maris said boldly. "They're supporting the Scottish rebels, I know it."

"We're not rehashing that debate." White said, sliding back into his chair, feigning normalcy despite the quickly-forming black eye he was sporting. "The Irish have pledged no support to the Scots. They're not our enemies."

Mordred was bored but he knew this was serious talk. In times like this his first instinct was to defer to the more vocal and brash members of his council: "Let's just send an army up there and shut them up? Sir Richard, you lead them."

"Very good your grace. I'll send word to Sir Oxlef."

"Why?"

"Because...as we discussed last week he was riding north with fifty men to meet with Sir Dondal at York. If we're bringing an army his way we should let him know."

THE LADY IN THE LAKE

"Oh yes, I, uh...forgot. Sir Oxlef, right. Then let's send a rook and tell him you're coming."

"Will his grace be riding out as well?" Sir Hanbury asked, feigning genuine interest but really playing games with no one in particular. Mordred didn't pick up on the sarcasm, however.

"Am I supposed to?"

"His grace will remain here." Sir Richard said tersely. "I think that adjourns the meeting, yes?"

"Y-yes." Mordred said as the group was already rising from their chairs to leave. "Sir Richard, wait a moment please."

The Knight lingered while the rest of the council dispersed. Mordred stood to address him properly. Even with his crown on, Arthur was still shorter by an inch. The tall Knight stood square-shouldered and straight-faced, a far cry from how he looked moments earlier when he had Sir White in a headlock on the floor. "I should apologize for my behavior during the meeting."

"Oh it's fine." Mordred said distantly.

"It is not, your grace, and I offer my sorry."

"Okay." Mordred said robotically. *He looks sad. I should frown.*

"Is there anything else?"

"Yes...do you think the Irish are plotting against us?"

"I think they are not to be trusted, not with that King Balor ruling them. They may be aiding the Scots, but they've yet to openly support them. Until they do, we've got other matters to address."

"Of course. And…you are on top of things?"

"I am, your grace."

"Shall I have Lord Lot go with you? He tends to speak on my behalf."

An awkward expression crossed over Richard's face, as it did whenever the son of Lord Baudwin came up to Sir Richard. Mordred—being terrible at reading reactions—wasn't sure what Richard's face meant and he was also too afraid to ask. "Lord Lot is not needed, if you understand my meaning. It's not my place to tell the King how to run his country or who should be the King's private counselors but since you asked I will say again…Lord Lot is not needed. I trust I am understood."

"Of course." Mordred lied. "Perfectly understood."

"Good." Richard said with a sigh of relief. "Then we'll speak no more of it. I am off, hopefully to return with a Kingdom that is whole once more."

"Thank you Sir Richard." Mordred said, remembering to smile at him. "Safe travels." he added, being especially proud that he remembered to say that, since he heard one of the Castle servants say it to him a few months ago when he went on holiday with his mother.

He watched the Knight stroll out of the

THE LADY IN THE LAKE

meeting room and, when the door closed behind him and Mordred was finally alone, his shoulders slumped, he fell in his chair and the pretense he'd been wearing like a cloak slipped off of him. *I hate this whole damned Kingdom*, he thought to himself and he meant every word: Mordred had long thought the Kingdom he inherited from his dead father was cursed—damned—and doomed to suffer every agonizing step of the way toward its own extinction. *If I am to lead it, I pray the end comes soon.*

*****

After a few minutes of much needed alone-time, Mordred left the council and headed toward the residence tower. Multiple aids and Castle staff passed him as he walked, but as his head was down he either did not see them or pretended not to see them. At the top of the tower his spacious room was waiting, too big for one man, with a wardrobe full of clothes and robes fit for a King, but still room left over, and with a bed beside the window, likewise too big for one man.

His door knocked-twice and his handmaid, Becka, entered. "Does his grace need anything at the moment?" she asked, careful not to make direct eye-contact, having learned the danger in doing so. Fortunately for her, Mordred was not looking her way; his eyes were on the window and to the wide-world that stretched beyond.

"Is my mother in the Castle?"

"She is, your grace."

"I'm going to see her." he said, before adding—just as Becka was about to disappear behind the door—"and have Rose meet me here when I return."

"Yes your grace." Becka said with a forlorn tone as she closed the door behind her.

She doesn't approve of Rose. Envious perhaps; I don't know, it looks the same as sadness sometimes and sometimes it looks like anger. Rose and I are in love and she can have no part of that.

*****

"And see to it that I have the notes on the meeting that just concluded." Gwen said as her door knocked twice. "Enter." she said before her aid could reach the door. In stepped Mordred, stripped down to trousers and a loose-fitting tunic. "Are you done for the day?" she asked him, noting his removal of every Kingly item of clothing. His blonde hair was a mess of curls, taken from his father (though Gwen was thankful the blonde came from Lancelot's appearance and not Kason—though the curls came from him—as it made it easier to pass him off as Arthur's child), and his piercing green eyes were a mirror of his mother's.

"The meeting adjourned less than an hour ago. We're apparently sending an army north to

THE LADY IN THE LAKE

quell the rebellion."

"Apparently? Didn't you give the order?"

"Oh, yes, of course. I gave the order."

"What's troubling you?"

"Nothing." he said, which was his go-to answer whenever anyone asked if something was wrong.

"I can tell you're upset."

"Really? How?" he asked. He was sincere in the question but it came off as combative. All his life he'd watched kids tell jokes and laugh and not understand. He'd see kids fall and scrape their knees and cry and not feel the slightest twinge of sympathy. He'd snatch butterflies from his window and rip the wings off, without the slightest regard for it. When the stablemaster's son wailed over his favorite horse having to be put down, Mordred only watched with morbid curiosity, not over the animal but the child who seemed so attached to it.

Even his own mother, who used to grip him close and squeeze him with her hugs, used to have to remind him to hug her back. *I suppose she didn't like having to do that,* he thought to himself. *Then again, no one asked me if I* wanted *a hug. I'd much rather—*

"Your grace, Rose is in your room." Becka said, her head sticking out of the door way for a fleeting moment before slamming it behind her.

"Rose? Still, Mordred?" Gwen said to him.

"Yes." he said defensively, unable to suppress the swelling of anger at his private life being examined. "What of it?"

"Don't you think you should concentrate on more important things than…"

"Than what?"

She sighed. "Don't you think you—"

"Than what?!" Mordred shouted, refusing to let her backpedal now.

"Than silly girls who will come when you call and only because you call. Because you are their King."

"You too? You and Becka both. You don't understand our relationship. Me and Rose, we—"

"There is no you and Rose. She doesn't—forget it. Go to her then."

"She does too." Mordred said, answering his mother's unfinished accusation. "More than you do."

"Excuse me?!" Gwen said, rising from her chair. She stood half a foot taller than him, not that it mattered. She put her eyes directly onto his and he wilted like a flower in the sun. "I **do** love you. More than you know. I love you enough to have protected you against all sorts of terrible things. You have no idea the things I've done to try…just to **try** and make you have a happy life." It was obvious there was a lot left unsaid, words and thoughts she'd been stewing over for maybe his entire life.

THE LADY IN THE LAKE

"Well don't stop now. Get it out!" he barked at his mother. She only stared at him, tears filling her eyes. "Why are you crying?" he snapped. Even in the middle of an argument, the instinct he'd developed over the years to ask his mother what all her emotions and emotional responses meant was too strong to ignore.

"You know why I'm crying." she said, wearily.

"No I don't. I don't know what that means!" he shouted, as he'd done countless times before.

"How can you not know by now!?" Gwen shouted back. "I'm crying because I'm sad. When people are sad they cry. That's what they do!"

"Well I've never been sad so I don't know!"

"You're always sad, Mordred! I don't blame you; you've never known you're father."

"No. That's why **you're** sad. I never knew him. I'm not sad he's dead; you are. For twenty years all I've heard about is this great King, so kind and so generous; all the people loved him, on and on and on and on. It's all a lie."

"What?" Gwen said breathlessly.

"A lie. All of it. If Arthur was so great, he'd have accomplished something. What did he do? There's nothing! I've read every scrap of parchment I could find and there's nothing he did of any note. Some battles and rebellions put down but mostly victories by great warriors; men he sent to fight for him."

"Says the King who has ordered an army to go North while he stays here and yells at his mother!"

smack

She tasted her own blood as it dripped from her bottom lip. He hadn't struck her in three years; she'd hoped that phase was behind him. He didn't apologize, nor did his face give any hint of suppressed remorse; that cut her deeper than his backhand. He might has well have been a statue. "I've read about everything he did as King, and as far as I can tell this Kingdom didn't lose much when it lost him. The King Kason before him at least accomplished—"

smack

He tasted his own blood.

"That man…" her finger was pointed at him, shaking. "was a disease. Twisted and cruel, who played with people like they were pawns, without remorse, without regard, with—" She stepped back from him, taking her eyes off his for the first time since he entered the room. "And not just this Kingdom, but the whole world is better with him dead."

"And yet…effective."

"How can you be so hateful? How can someone who doesn't even know what the

THE LADY IN THE LAKE

happiness or anger or sadness on my face even means be so skilled at hate? Above all emotions, why is that the one you've managed to master."

He did not respond; there was nothing else to say. They'd had fights like this at least once every few months. He would bottle his feelings up and then release them on the one person who would take them. It was just a routine to him, as ordinary as getting dressed in the morning or eating dinner at night.

The moment was ended, the fight was finished; Mordred turned to the room's exit. "Where are you going?" his mother called to him, mostly in frustration though a hint of regret was there to be heard if you had the capacity to hear it.

"To my room right now. To Rose…and then tomorrow to Edinburgh."

"Edinburgh?"

"I'm going to lead the army." He said the words spontaneously, which was not at all like the careful planner he was. Mordred was the kind of young man who would rehearse various conversations in his head, planning what answers he'd give should some question come to him, always prepared with a prepared answer. But here he was speaking rashly. *Is that an emotion?* he wondered.

"I'm sorry I said those things, Mordred. Please, don't go off to—"

"No you're right. It's wrong of me to

criticize my father who never led a battle a day in his life."

"That's not true—"

"So I'll go in the name of the Kings who ruled **before** my father and I'll lead the battle and put down the rebellion of the Scots."

"You're not...are you sure you're ready?" she asked, now fighting back tears for an entirely different reason.

"I'm the King. I was born ready." he lied. The words sounded stupid coming from his lips, but he'd heard one of his Knights say something similarly and everyone around made noises that seemed like they were impressed by it. His mother did not make those noises, however. "Would you like me to kiss and hug you tomorrow before I leave?"

"Yes." she said weakly, too tired to fight him any more, too tired even to be proud of him for knowing at least to ask instead of having to be told to do that before leaving. He closed the door behind her and she crumpled to her chair, suddenly exhausted and completely defeated. *What a child I have...* she thought sadly to herself.

*****

Rose was waiting for him, sitting awkwardly on the edge of the bed, eyes locked onto the window even as the door opened and Mordred entered. He immediately ran to his chamber pot to

THE LADY IN THE LAKE

hurl.

He doesn't typically do that.

"Are you...okay?" Rose asked. This was not her first time in Mordred's room and though they were usually filled with awkward moments, she couldn't think of a time when he went straight from the door to the toilet.

"I'm going to Edinburgh tomorrow." he groaned in between heaves.

"To the Rebellion? That doesn't sound like you." she said, blurting out the last bit before she could stop herself.

"I know! I need to think. I'm sorry I don't think we can have dinner together tonight."

"Oh—okay sure." Rose said, careful not to tip off how relieved she was to hear that.

"You're not mad?"

"No, it's fine. You're busy."

"Should you be mad?"

"Um...No?"

"Okay, I'm glad." he said, remembering to smile as he slowly climbed off the floor. "I promise we'll spend time together when I get back."

"That's...great; that'll be really great." she said flatly as she hurried to scoot off the bed and get out of the room before he changed his mind. The door flung open before she reached it and his mother burst in.

"News." Gwen said, holding a roll of

parchment. The seal was already broken and the panic in her eyes indicated she was the one who'd read the word before her son. Mordred didn't even bother to read it.

"What does it say?"

"The Irish." she said, holding out the roll of paper for him to take; he did not.

"They've announced their support for the Scots?" Mordred asked lazily.

"They've **joined** the Scots." She unrolled the parchment and read it aloud. "A fleet of ships bearing some twenty-thousand footmen, archers, and destriers have landed at Irvine and by now would have reached Glasgow." she stopped speaking but her eyes kept moving, back and forth across the ink, looking for some word of comfort or a not of relief; there was none. Finally she lifted her eyes to look at her son, the color now completely drained from his face. *He looks so much like a boy, so unready for all of this.*

"Well..." he mumbled, before beginning to pace. "Clearly we need to delay or arrival at Edinburgh; if we march in now they'll bring the fullness of their, uh... combined forces you know...against us." He nodded to himself, satisfied that he'd said something that sounded halfway-intelligent, and looked to his mother (by instinct) for approval.

"You need to remain here." Gwen said flatly. "Have your forces camp at York to defend

THE LADY IN THE LAKE

against invasion."

"There's no evidence of an inv—"

"They didn't land twenty-thousand soldiers on our soil for a game of bowling!" Gwen tossed the parchment down in a gesture that she'd intended to be a punctuation mark to her shouting, but instead it just fluttered and twisted as it slowly glided down to the ground. For a moment, everyone watched it, mesmerized, until Mordred finally retorted.

"It's not our soil, it's the Scots'." he said.

"What?" Gwen scoffed. "It's your soil; you are the King of this whole Great Island. The Scots have no right to rebel and the Irish have no right to invade. You need to send your forces to York—"

"Well then why haven't you done it!?"

"Because I'm standing here being yelled at by you! …Where are **you** going?!" he shouted over his mother's shoulder to Rose as she was **just** about to slip out the door.

"Oh I was just…"

"You're not leaving." Mordred snapped, eyes as relaxed and emotionless as ever though his tone was manic. "Nobody's leaving. Not until we have figured out a strategy."

"Come on." Gwen said to Rose as she spun around for the door.

"What—?" Mordred was incredulous.

"You're not having a war strategy with your mother and a handmaid. Call your council."

"My council already met today. They don't meet again till—"

"Call them again, Mordred. Make them come. Be the King." She didn't want to dress him down, especially not in front of others, but her mother's instinct took over. "You can at least do that." she added, instantly regretting her word choice and tone. Fortunately for her, Mordred did not pick up on the tone. Unfortunately for her, Rose did and her reaction (a wide-mouthed look of shock to her someone speak to the King so disrespectfully) **was** noticed by Mordred.

"I don't know what that means, so just tell me what to do."

She sighed, weary from the day, if not the past twenty years. "You must fight them, but you also must win. If you don't fight you embolden them. If you lose…you might lose everything. *He'd just as soon surrender the north to the Scots; anything to avoid doing…anything.*

He tore away from her piercing green gaze and focused on Rose. After a few seconds she finally looked up to see him. "Call a meeting with the War Council. We'll discuss strategy as we ride."

"Ride?" Gwen asked.

"I'm going to York or Edinburgh or wherever." he answered, exuding none of the confidence needed to inspire a General, or an army, or anyone.

THE LADY IN THE LAKE

Gwen walked out of the room almost in a trance. The door closed behind her and she was halfway down the spiral stairway of the King's tower before she realized her son was a week away from either losing his life or the whole kingdom. *And I can't honestly say which would be worse,* she thought, before cursing herself for thinking it.

MATTHEW L. MARTIN
CHAPTER 4 : SURPRISE

There was some debate amongst Eric's crew about what to do with the carriage they had decided to take to meet O'Mare's business associate. After the bar fight was ended and the dust settled, Eric knew they needed to get out of town, for Raph's sake as much as their own. "The Inquisitor's is **right here**!" Eric said, against Marcalla's protests.

She naturally thought stealing the ride from the people you just killed was bad karma but they took a vote and the "ayes" had it. The fact that it was painted with a big giant red cross was a problem that needed to be addressed immediately, however.

THE LADY IN THE LAKE

Jay thought they should dump it as soon as possible and swap it out for something less conspicuous ("The last thing we need is anyone asking questions!"). Petro thought a simple coat of paint would be sufficient to keep them out of trouble ("We'll tell people we bought it used and touched it up."). Fortigo had no opinion. Dun never had an opinion. Marcella was too busy arguing with Eric about it to settle on what to do.

"I can't believe you're still mad." Eric said, sitting to Marcella's left behind the horses that pulled them toward Grenoble.

Marcella shook her head in disbelief. "You didn't have to kill him."

"There were quite a few swords pointed at me, actually; which one didn't I have to kill?"

"Don't be dumb. He was just a kid."

"Don't do that." Eric said, warningly.

"Do what?"

"Start giving backstories to people like that."

"He was half your age, if not younger. Young enough to be your own son."

"Whoa, out of bounds."

"My point is—"

"I know your point. You looked up and saw his pretty face and felt bad for him."

"Well not at first. I felt bad when you shoved a knife in his chest."

"I was aiming for that red cross he was wearing. **You** saw his face; **I** never took my eyes off his emblem."

"It's been twenty years."

"Nope. Don't do that either." Eric said tersely.

"Well we have another two days to Grenoble. We can talk about nothing or we can talk about—"

"Does someone want to switch seats with Marcella!" he shouted to the gang in the wagon behind him. No one responded; they were all content to obviously eavesdrop.

"I'm going to say my peace." Marcella said, with a commanding, final sort of tone that Eric knew quite well not to argue with. It was part of what attracted him to her, the way she looked at him like an equal to spar with, not just a lover to cuddle with.

"Fine say it, but it's not going end with me saying I shouldn't have killed that k—Templar."

"Twenty years ago you lost your King, lost your friends, lost your home…and you blame the Templar."

"With good reason!" Eric scoffed.

"I'm not done. You blame the Templar because it's easier to blame them than to blame the people who command them. You can't kill the Pope, you can't kill the witch or whoever it was that send that headless giant, but you can hunt Templar down. And you did."

"Yes I did." he said without a hint of

remorse.

"Yes you did. For ten years you did. I don't know how they didn't catch you and kill you ten times over, but you survived. And then I came along."

"Is this going to end with your asking me to marry you again?"

"I came along," she said, ignoring his snark, "and led you down a different path. A better one."

"Yes. Smuggling and mercenary work: Much more noble."

"The point is you spent ten years trying to take your anger out on people who didn't kill your King or your friends or take any of that life away from you. They just wear the same shirt. And after ten years what did it get you? Nothing. You were just as bitter and suicidal as ever."

"I wasn't suicidal…"

"You crashed into Templar meeting house and set the whole thing on fire while a dozen of them swarmed you. You had Samson-like tendencies."

"Fine."

"I take the credit for bringing you out of your funk. It wasn't killing Templar that did it, it was me. Now I want you to give me something in return: Let it go. You can't change the past and can't bring them back. Just let go of your hate and look to the future…" She let her words hang for a moment, giving them time to sink in before adding, "and marry me already."

"Look out!" Jay shouted from the back. Eric pulled the reins just in time; a man in the road ahead only **just** dove out of their path, a half-second before being run over. Marcella leapt onto the road to check, returning a moment later with a man looking positively shaken, wide-eyed and breathing quick, short gasps.

"You okay?" Eric asked.

"I guess I am." he said feebly. He stood only a little shorter than Marcella, and looked a fair bit younger too; mid-twenties by the look of him. His dark skin gave no hint of his nationality, and he wore only common clothes with no insignia or other noteworthy emblems.

"This is a lonely road to be travelling on foot." Petro said with his faux-"wise old Asian mystic" affectation. "Where is your horse?"

"Broken leg yesterday. Been walking ever since."

"Where are you going?" Marcella asked him.

"Where are **you** going?" he returned the question.

"Grenoble!" Jay said. The annoyed looks on the faces of his companions indicated they didn't want to reveal that information.

"Then so am I…if you'll have me."

"No." Eric said. "We don't know you. Why would we let you come along."

THE LADY IN THE LAKE

"Because it's the right thing to do?" Jay said. Even Marcella seemed to be leaning in that direction.

"Where **were** you going when your horse broke down." Eric asked him.

"Back to my home…" His eyes shifted around the group of them, uncomfortably.

"You're going to have to do better than that."

"I am of Rome." he blurted. "Please do not attack me, I have no weapons!"

"He's clean, I checked." Marcella said, noticing Eric's question to her with his eyes.

"I was here travelling for leisure and was on my way home. I live in a village just on the other side of the border."

"Alright, get in." Marcella said, much to Eric's surprise.

"Thank you, thank you all. I'm Sal." He looked back to smile at the rest of the group but only Jay and Fortigo returned the gesture. "Are you…a family?"

"No." Eric said quickly before Jay could say otherwise.

*****

As the sun's last light was disappearing over the horizon, their carriage arrived at a small town about a day's journey from Grenoble. "Inn." Marcella said, pointing over to a tall building off the rod. "You want me to get us a few rooms?" she asked as they pulled their carriage to a stop in front of the three-story structure.

"No, you keep an eye on...everything." Eric replied, darting his eye quickly to Sal before hopping out and strolling inside.

"So..." Sal smiled stupidly at Fortigo and Dun. The former was twiddling his thumbs quietly while the later was sleeping (and, judging by the quick jerks he was making, having a nightmare). "How did you two...meet?"

Fortigo flashed a large grin, apparently delighted to tell the tale. "Oh it's a funny story!" he said, jubilantly.

"It's really not." Jay whispered.

"I used to sell shoes." Fortigo said, punctuating his comment with a nod as though his story was done.

"...is that it?" Sal asked.

"Oh, uh...no. It's just usually when I tell the story people stop to laugh when I tell them I used to sell shoes." He paused again, as though waiting for Sal to laugh. He did not.

"Please continue."

"Right, so anyway, one day in comes this guy, tall and lanky with this little rascal here on his back." He rubbed Dun's spiky black hair, waking the little man up and just missing having his finger bitten. "He—the guy I mean, not Dun here—he was looking for shoes so I helped him out. He

THE LADY IN THE LAKE

didn't seem to like my shoes so he left but he left these." Fortigo flashed a pair of golden bracelets he was wearing on his wrists. Gemstones of white were embedded in the bands and Dun looked at them with obvious longing.

"You stole his bracelets?"

"What? No, he died. Got hit by a cow."

"…"

"I ran out to help but he was a goner. Dun here was thrown a good bit away, wailing in pain. I couldn't just leave him, the little tyke, and I felt like the whole thing was my fault, me not havin' the right shoes and all, making his master leave the shop right as that cow was running wild down the road…so I scooped him up and pledged my life to him, promising to help him along the way."

"Wow that's…that's…you got a story, that's for sure."

"And magic bracelets." Fortigo said matter of factly.

"Magic?"

"Yeah the guy, the one hit by the cow? He was a wizard or something. His bracelets do all kinds of spells, well look what it did for me!" he said plainly, as though it was obvious.

Sal looked to Jay for an explanation but the young man had none, though he did have a theory he was happy to whisper: "He never takes the bracelets off but my theory is if he did, Fortigo would turn into a scrawny little twerp like me and

Dun would become a giant."

"I'm going to help Eric." Marcella finally sighed, weary from the conversation behind her. As she entered the Inn she immediately wished she'd insisted on being the one to haggle with the innkeeper. Eric and he were in the middle of a shouting match.

"You're throwing money away!" Eric barked, slamming his palm on the counter.

"I do not care." the man retorted.

"How can you not?! You have three rooms but you won't let us rent any of them on the off chance someone else comes along! We're here! We've come along!"

"It does not matter." The inn-keeper was displaying remarkable patience, despite the much larger Eric leaning over the counter into his personal space. "We have a troupe of travelling acrobats that always stay here when they are passing through; those rooms are kept open for them. I'm sorry."

"This is terrible customer service!"

"It is not."

"How is it not?!"

"You are not a customer." he shrugged, supremely satisfied with his witty retort. "On the contrary our guests are always treated quite well."

"Come on, we'll ride straight on and take turns driving." Marcella said, pulling Eric back by the arm.

THE LADY IN THE LAKE

They climbed back into the wagon just as the rest of their party were starting to climb out. "Get back in, we're going." he snapped.

"No room?" Jay asked.

"Yes room, no good." Eric grumbled as he snapped the reins and left the town. They rode through the night, Eric trading placing with Marcella who traded places with Jay, who quickly traded places with Eric again when he woke up and saw Jay was driving.

Late into the next day they reached Grenoble. "We're here." Sal said. "There's a church a little ways ahead. You can find what you're looking for there."

"What are we looking for?" Eric asked him, warily.

"Mr. Graves, right?" Sal said, prompting Eric to stop the ride immediately.

"I didn't mention Graves." Eric said. Marcella shook her head as well. "Start talking."

"Why don't you take us to the church and I'll let him explain everything."

The church in question was a modest structure, wider than it was deep with a steeple rising above the only visible doorway. Its red and black brickwork was a stark contrast to the rest of the wooden buildings around town. More curious was the utter lack of any passers-by walking near the building. Everyone in town seemed content to keep their distance from it, despite it being the only building with a steeple they could see.

"What am I going to find when I go in there?" Eric asked, his hand already gripping his sword's hilt. "A dozen Templar."

"Temp—ha!" Sal barked a laugh. "Hardly. No, you'll find something else entirely."

"Stop being cryptic." Eric snapped. "We gave you a lift here and you were obviously waiting for us. Who are you and who is in that—" He turned his face to the church, finger pointed at the door, which was now open revealing the priest standing on the top step outside. He was a gangly-thin old man, with tufts of white hair coming out of his black head. Clearly a priest, the man wore ornate robes with a white cross etched on to them, but instead of a dull black he wore garments of powder blue. Eric recognized him immediately, despite how long it'd been since he'd laid eyes on him.

"It's our dad, Eric." Sal said to him. Eric turned back to the stranger he'd only just met yesterday, not bothering to hide the look that couldn't decide between anger and confusion; either way his look seemed out of place on a face with such watery eyes. "Surprise."

THE LADY IN THE LAKE

MATTHEW L. MARTIN
CHAPTER 5 : LEAVE NO DOUBT

His head was swimming, his eyes were ringing and his eyes could not focus, but when Arthur inhaled the cool air of his surroundings, he felt the rush of life course through his body, and there is nothing quite as magical. "He's awake." he heard a woman say...and not just any woman; **the** woman, the one who came to bring him back.

"I'm not going to linger." another voice answered. *Corvis,* he knew.

"I can't see." Arthur said, raising a shaky hand to his face. "At least not well." he added as the dull grey blur of his surroundings filled with the blurry lightness of his hand in front of his eyes.

"It'll all come back soon." The Lady replied.

"Your body hasn't been used in a while. Give it a minute to remember how to focus the eyes."

"Where am I?"

"Merlin's house in France."

"Under France." Corvis said, correcting her.

"Yes we're under a lake in the middle of France. Merlin does like his hiding places and this is a good one."

"Is he here?"

"No, he is away." Behind her Corvis *harrumphed.* "He is off recruiting for the coming fight. Which is why you're here."

"How long again did you say…I mean, how long have I been away?"

"About twenty years." The Lady said. Her voice filled his right ear and her cool and pleasant hand rested on his wrist. "Things have changed somewhat, but some things are mostly as you left it."

"Gwen." he said. It was neither a question nor a request, just a audible mention of the woman he'd left.

"She is…still in England. You'll see her soon." The Lady's tone was undeniable; Arthur had used a similar one more times than he could count. He knew what it sounded like when someone was trying to keep an uncomfortable truth from being spoken while also not outright lying about it. What he didn't know was what exactly the uncomfortable truth was.

"I only just realized there's a lot I don't know." Arthur said awkwardly. "Why specifically did you bring me back. What good can I be?"

"The fight ahead will need men and women of exceptional character." she answered.

"Right, well character I may have but I'm no good in a fight." He rubbed his hand across his midsection, only half-expecting to feel some reminder of the gash that had stopped him dead in his tracks at the Tree of Knowledge years ago. Instead he felt nothing out of the ordinary. "Am I in my own body?" he asked suddenly. It was a silly question, he knew, but one he needed to ask if only to settle the nagging questions he had about his bring brought back.

"Your body was cast into the Great Sea by the Librarian." The Lady answered, her voice ever so slightly unsteady. "The rest of you has been with Corvis. We recovered your body but it was greatly decayed."

"That doesn't really answer my question."

"You are you, yes." she said flatly. "Parts of you are twenty years older, other parts haven't aged a week, but you are you."

"So, about your plan for me then?"

"Morgana is amassing an army. We don't know where, nor do we know what kind of army it is. She may have infiltrated Rome. She may have secured enough power to wield the dead. There is much we don't know."

THE LADY IN THE LAKE

"I thought you people had all the answers?"

"My sister is very cunning and powerful herself. This is not the first time she's disappeared from my sight. Wherever she is, she does not want to be seen and so she will not be until she strikes."

"I'm not going to be much help to you." Arthur confessed. "I know you think I'm some great hero and leader, mighty King and all, but—"

"Oh Arthur. No one thinks you're mighty. And for the most part you've never demonstrated great heroism."

"Well…" Suddenly he felt the need to defend himself though his counter-arguments were coming up blank.

"You lack almost every quality needed to be an effective King." Her tone was not cutting or rebuking, but simply pitiable. She might as well have added a "bless your heart" to the front of it.

"Alright, well you wanted me." Arthur said, more than a little annoyed.

"Yes. Because though you lack many of the qualities most would look for in a hero, you possess the one quality that counts the most, the one quality that few think to look for. You have the one quality that is in short supply these days."

"And that is?"

"Fidelity."

"Fi—are you serious? You think I'm faithful?"

"I know you are."

"I don't think you've done your homework." He slowly sat up from the bed he was laying on, then nearly flopped back down when his blurred vision began to darken. Faint orange balls were glowing on either side of him, the blurrily-seen light of twin burning candles that illuminated the shimmering blue dress and vivid silver hair of The Lady in front of him. Behind her he could make out a slender white blob; Corvis was not saying much but he hadn't left yet either.

"Arthur there have been…I can't even say how many guardians and other people like me who have come to your world to labor and help. Not all of them have kept the faith; in fact several gone the way of Morgana at one time or another. The power we wield is extraordinary and the temptation to abuse it equally so. To be a King also means to hold great power and there have been many to wear a crown who have misused it or simply been crushed under the weight of it. But you have not."

"Well I've been dead, so…"

"No, you ruled nobly. Were you the fiercest or the most awe-inspiring? No. But you were just, kind and fair, and never swayed by the desire to have more and more power."

Arthur could only scoff. "I'm sorry but you have me all wrong. I mean, all that you said is sort of true but it's not the way you're presenting it. You're making me out to be some paradigm of

THE LADY IN THE LAKE

virtue and benevolence when really I just hate confrontation. I'm not special; I'm weak. I'm not remarkably faithful or anything; I'm just a coward. I sort of fell backwards into all of this. I didn't even want to pull that stupid sword!" He blurted the last line almost by instinct.

"But the sword wanted you." she said. "Morgana made it, I placed it there, Merlin enchanted it. We all had our part to play, but the sword wanted you."

"I imagine it wants to return to its owner."

"No…she wants it very badly I suspect, but it's happy where it is." She raised a hand toward the wall next to her. Arthur's eyes followed her movements and fell upon the ruby handle of Excalibur. His vision cleared like a lifting fog and the room came into sharp focus. The rest of the blade was hidden, buried under an assortment of parchment scraps and hastily placed shields and weapons, but that distinctive handle and crossguard was unmistakable.

"So what am I supposed to do?"

"England needs her King—" The Lady began to say, but her words were cut off by Corvis, who stepped forward into view.

"England has a King." the man in white said sternly. "I told you I don't approve of this, Vivianne—"

"Then there's no need to tell me again, Corvis." she responded softly.

"My son..." Arthur mumbled, putting it together who the current King must be. "I've missed his whole childhood and now he's ruling."

"Well he's the King," The Lady corrected him, "I wouldn't say he's ruling."

"What does that mean?"

"He lacks his father's...instincts." she answered rather cryptically, though clearly she had more on her mind than she was telling him. "I'll tell you more tomorrow. Sleep now." She placed a hand on his forehead and immediately he felt groggy. The urge to lie back down quickly supplanted the desire to ask more questions. He fell back against the soft bed, and his eyes closed. He could hear The Lady and Corvis continuing their argument, but the voices were drifting away from him...

*****

"Arthur..." *I know that voice*, he thought to himself. "Wake up. We have a big day today."

He opened his eyes to see the face he'd been missing since...forever. Hair as red as fire and eyes so green they almost glowed, Gwen looked exactly like she did the last time he saw her. "What is today?" he asked, groggily. He felt like he'd been sleeping for three days straight.

"My birthday!" she said with a playful punch to his arm. "You said we'd go to see that soothsayer in Kent.

THE LADY IN THE LAKE

"The one with the crazy hair…" He said the words as though he knew exactly what she was talking about, and the more he thought about it the more certain he was he **did** know. All the other questions he had were quickly vanishing the way memories of a dream do.

"What about Corvis?" he said, grasping at the only thing from his dream he could remember.

"If you want to invite him, I guess you can. He'd be better off here tending the sheep, don't you think?"

"Right, our sheep." he said, shaking the cobwebs out of his head. "We have sheep."

"Well yeah, how else we supposed to make a living?" she snorted and slipped out of bed. Arthur took the moment to examine his surroundings; *this is our cottage*, he told himself, almost as if to assure himself of it. *We live here with…* "Adam." he said, knowing the name immediately.

"He's still asleep." she replied casually. "He better be after keeping me up all night nursing."

She disappeared out of the bedroom and returned a moment later with a boy of bright red hair, sleeping soundly in her arms. "He's so adorable…let's wake him up!" Arthur said playfully, reaching for him as Gwen pulled him back, desperate to keep him asleep.

"Isn't this nice?" she said.

"It is. It's like…"

"All you ever wanted. Peace and quiet, a family, a little farm to do you work, nothing to worry about. Just let someone else handle the big things. That's not for you anyway."

"It really isn't." he agreed, but though the words came out of his mouth they didn't seem to originate within him. They came from somewhere else, somewhere elusive and unidentifiable. "Who is the King?" he said, speaking words that **did** come from within him, although they had to be forced into focus from a mind that seemed very cloudy.

It was as if there was a fog filling half his head; above it were the pleasant and dream-like thoughts of a happy life with Gwen and Adam. Underneath were the obscured ideas and memories that he couldn't quite see but which he could will to the surface.

"What?" Gwen asked him.

"Who is the King?"

She furrowed her brow. "There is no King. The Lords govern the land if that's what you mean. Unless you mean the Empress, but she's in Rome."

"The Empress…"

"Where is the sword?" she asked suddenly. Her tone was casual, but the subject matter was oddly disconnected from what they'd been talking about.

"My sword?"

THE LADY IN THE LAKE

"Yes. Think Arthur. Just…where is it? I know it's in this house somewhere. Do you remember where you hid it; I can't find it anywhere."

"Did you check the armory?" he asked stupidly, not sure where that idea came from other than deep within his mind.

"We don't have an armory. You're not the King. This is just a cottage house. Where might it be? Is there a secret room? Where did my sister put it?"

"I don't, uh…"

"Arthur look at me." He turned his eyes toward her striking green stare. The black of her pupils was gone, the white of her eyes flooded with emerald-green as well. Staring into them seemed to wash away all the confusion and conflicted thoughts he was having. "This life is as real as you could ever need it to be. All you need to do is just give me my sword."

"I haven't had it since the library." he answered, hypnotized by her gaze.

"Yes. the Librarian sent it to my sister."

"Your sister is…The Lady." He blinked and in the split second that followed, his wife's beautiful face was replaced by another, sickly and pale, yet clearly beautiful once upon a time. Her black hair floated above her head like she was under water. "I know you…"

"No, what do you mean?" she said. It was

MATTHEW L. MARTIN

Gwen's voice. He blinked again and it was Gwen's face in front of him.

"No…"

"Arthur don't think, just say what you know. Where is the sword."

"No this is not real. This is something else." Instantly her hand was wrapped around his heart, squeezing him.

"Let him go." Another voice called out. "Let him go and I will give you the sword."

"Don't lie, sister. It's not becoming."

"I swear it."

With a cold gasp he inhaled sharply, feeling Morgana's grip relax from his chest. "Do it." she said.

Fingers wrapped around Arthur's wrist. He looked down to see a woman's hand. He followed it up with his eyes, from her wrist to her elbow to her shoulder to her face—

He woke up.

"There. You see? Fidelity." The Lady said. She wasn't speaking to Arthur. He wanted to turn his head to see the one she was looking at but his muscles were frozen. He put two and two together fairly quickly, however.

"She wants the sword." Arthur said, stupidly.

"It's my sword." Morgana sneered.

"Let him go," The Lady said, "he turned

THE LADY IN THE LAKE

your offer down. He's of no value to you now."

"Give it to me like you promised, Vivianne."

"Let me send him away and I will give you the sword."

Morgana scoffed. "All my life you have tried to put me in my place, tell me what to do and how to live. You've always tried to make the rules for me. Now here you are, when I have all the power, you still can't help yourself but to make more and more rules. You made a promise; live up to it. No more making rules."

"If by that you mean I have looked after you, yes. I've tried to help you, even when you went your own way."

"You call it help; I call it control. And now I'm done talking about it." A shockwave ripped through Arthur, erupting out of Morgana and exploding the house around them. Instantly he felt the hold over him break but out of both fear and confusion he remained where he was. He looked around to see the dark blue of a lakebed all around him, with a bubble of air encasing the remnants of the destroyed house.

The debris floated in place, seemingly suspended by Morgana's outstretched hand. With her other hand the black-haired witch sent The Lady tumbling backwards away from them, breaking through the air bubble into the lake beyond. "There." Morgana said, finding the sword amongst the floating wreckage.

Arthur dove for it but she was faster. Her fingers wrapped around the ruby hilt and the rainbow band that danced up and down the blade coursed under her skin. She inhaled a slow, deep breath of pure ecstasy. "I made this, a long time ago, because your ancestor seemed the conquering type. He was a disappointment. His son was an even bigger one. Now there's you and your brother."

"What?" Arthur asked.

You think because you pulled it out of a chair that it belongs to you?"

"No." Arthur said, speaking honestly, mind still racing with what she'd just said about...a brother? *What brother. I have no brother.* His thoughts filled with memories, flashes of images and sounds he'd long set aside. There was always ever his father and mother, and when she died, his father only. *There was Kason; he was like a brother once. And The Lady Elaine, she was always like a second mother, the way she opened their home up to he and his father whenever Wilheim was away...oh my—*

Morgana pointed the blade at him, jolting him back to the present moment. "My sister seems to think you're important. I was never much for seeing the future. What do you think? Think you're worth keeping alive?"

"No." Arthur said, again honestly but again only half paying attention, despite the seriousness of the moment. *I have a brother. Does Kason know?*

THE LADY IN THE LAKE

Surely he's dead.

The Lady's voice filled the space between Morgana and Arthur and again he returned to the present situation: "I **have** seen the future, sister. And it ends with his life and your death."

Morgana's face remained stiff and expressionless. She nodded slightly in response to The Lady's remarks, keeping her eyes focused on Arthur, who stared back at her with as much severity and intensity as he could muster. "Maybe." she replied. "But the future maybe isn't as set in stone as you'd like it to be."

Excalibur slashed through the air, left and right, up and down, twisting and jabbing with inhuman speed. Morgana wielded it like an extension of herself, a longer arm with a pointed tip that sliced Arthur's body into innumerable pieces. He did not even scream; there was no time. He was cut and killed faster than in the blink of an eye.

Morgana looked over the ruined remains of Arthur with a mixture of boredom and temerity. The power of Excalibur was finally reunited with its maker and she, stronger than ever, needed only to flick her fingers in his direction to explode him into an infinite number of pieces. Arthur was gone, evaporated, utterly destroyed, completely dead.

"Now then...the real work begins." Morgana said with a sigh as she disappeared, leaving behind no physical trace of Arthur. But then again there are some things that aren't physical.

And those things **exist** without a trace, don't they?

THE LADY IN THE LAKE

MATTHEW L. MARTIN
CHAPTER 6 : THE WIZARD AND THE CROOK

He towered over the gnome-like man—if he could even be called a man—seething in rage and desperate to land a punch. With every swing, however, Kerem missed his target entirely. It was not for lack of skill, however. Rumpel simply had better timing; he zipped around the room, blinking in and out of space and time an instant before Kerem's massive fist would have driven into his face.

"Hold still and tell the truth!" Kerem shouted in frustration.

"I've never been good at either of those things." Rumpel said, allowing himself a few seconds to smile at Kerem's exasperated anger.

THE LADY IN THE LAKE

"Up here." he said, drawing the large Turk's attention to the mantelpiece above the fireplace. Kerem dove for him but Rumpel, once again, simply disappeared faster than a blink, reappearing on the sofa on the other side of the room. Kerem's fist crashed into the mantle, rattling a few gold bars that were perched on top.

"Where did you get the gold?!" he shouted again.

"I told you when I met you not to worry about it."

"You didn't say anything about the Vizier's men banging on my door in the middle of the night!"

"It's not his gold, don't worry about him." Rumpel lied with a dismissive wave. "I told you...well, first I told you not to ask, then I told you it came from nowhere." He vanished again and reappeared back on the mantel, sitting next to a stack of gold bricks with his stubby legs dangling happily over the edge. "You can chase me around your living room all day if you want; you'll get tired but I won't."

"Or?"

"Or you can stop and give me what you promised me and you'll never have to see me again."

"The deal's off, troll."

"Watch it...you. Sorry, there's no epithet for people who are tall, dark and handsome like yourself."

"Flattery?"

"I told you I'm no good at telling the truth. Listen, we had an agreement. I did my part, now you do—"

"No. You said the gold would come from nowhere."

"And so it did." Rumpel said, struggling to pick up one of the gold bars next to him. "Shiny and fresh." He took a great inhale, like a smoker admiring a cigar. "Delightful."

"No, it did not come from nowhere. I did some thinking."

"Oh that's never a good idea."

"You can't get gold from nowhere; you can't get anything from nowhere."

"Why is that?"

"Because if you could, it would mean that nowhere at one time had gold to be gotten from."

"Don't hurt yourself trying to work this all out, now." Rumpel said, noticing Kerem's very pained look as he tried to remember the details of his conclusion.

"If you got gold from nowhere that means nowhere used to be place with gold, which means it was a somewhere…a somewhere that had lots of gold. So if nowhere was a somewhere then it couldn't have been a nowhere, which means you're a liar and that gold is stolen."

"I'm not going to lie…your logic is sound."

THE LADY IN THE LAKE

He hopped up and shrugged, looking not a bit sympathetic. "What do you want me to do? Turn your gold back into straw? What fun would that be? I still did what we agreed on, you still owe a barrel of your wine."

"I said no deal. You lied, the deal's off."

Now it was Rumpel showing signs of frustration. "Why are you so difficult? No one else has ever given me such grief about free money! I just want a barrel; one measly little barrel. Don't make me go to brewer two towns over; you know you have the best stuff."

"Here's what's going to happen, troll. I'm going to go to the bathroom. I'm taking this newsparchment to read. When it's done, I'll be done. And when I step back in my living room, I want that gold back where the Vizier had it and I want my straw back where I had it—"

"You could have left off the whole first part of this speech."

"—And I want you gone."

"A mulligan, a do-over, a hard reset." Rumpel said, nodding his head. "That's fair. You drive a hard bargain my large Turkish friend. I'll take all your gold away and give you back all your straw…for one barrel of wine."

Kerem did not retort; he only scowled at him and exited his house (off to his outhouse, but you didn't need to know that part). The moment the door shut, Rumpel hopped off the mantle and looked left and right. He rummaged under loose parchments, tossed-about books and other clutter, searching for…

"Got em." he said, holding up an iron ring of keys. Quickly he scurried to the back of Kerem's house, unlocked the several locks that secured an old iron door and scrambled down the stairway to the darkened cellar below. A minute or two passed before any other sound was heard in the house. Finally a *clunk, clu-clunk, clu-clunk* echoed up the stairway, as Rumple slowly rolled the large barrel of wine up to the first floor.

Slowly he rolled the barrel down the hallway and back to the sitting room, toward the front door and to the world outside; a world filled with more men, women and families to con. "Don't judge me," Rumpel said to the narrator. "We all have to make a living. And I'm—"

"I forgot my newspa—" Kerem was bent over, belt undone with one hand holding his pants up and the other reaching for the newsparchment on the table. For a quiet moment the two stared at each other, with Rumpel quickly debating if he should abandon his wine or try and figure out a way to get it **and** himself out of there, and Kerem (slowly) figuring out that Rumpel had no intention of returning the gold he had stolen for him but was instead trying to make off with his prized wine.

Finally Rumpel spoke: "I can see the wheels turning behind your eyes, Kerem, so let me just do

THE LADY IN THE LAKE

this..." Slowly he pulled out of hip flask in one hand and a wand in the other. With a tap-tap he touched the side of the barrel with his wand and immediately a jet of scarlet began pouring out of the side, which he promptly caught in the opening of his flask. After a moment, the container was full.

It was around that time that Kerem (finally) figured out what was happening and charged for him. For once, the gnome-like man was caught off guard. Forgetting to just disappear, he instead zipped around the barrel, slipping on the still-pouring wine, and slid under the Turk's long legs. He was out the door right around the time Kerem also slipped on the wine, crashing to the floor and providing Rumpel ample time to escape down the road.

He bounded down the dirty road, away from the cottage that was isolated from the rest of the town. He was half a day's ride from Istanbul but he might as well have been in the middle of nowhere there were so few people around. *Still, it was a worthwhile con,* he thought to himself as he gripped his flask. *Pity I couldn't take the whole barrel.*

"Penny for the poor?" a feeble voice rang out, stopping Rumpel dead in his tracks.

Rumpel didn't hear him but saw, from the corner of his beady little eye, a beggar's hand extending toward him. He stopped a few yards away from him and looked back at the pathetic man inquisitively. "What did you say?" his gravelly, almost growling voice asked. All the playfulness he had with Kerem was replaced by something much more sinister for this stranger.

The beggar, finally getting a good look at the short troll, scooted back a few feet. If he had any strength in his legs, he would have leapt up and fled. "I—I—I'm so hungry." he said, with the bottle he had tied to a string around his neck looking more than half full.

"Are you?" Rumpel said, looking almost amused by the beggar's plight. His eyes caught sight of the bottle and he smacked his lips instinctively.

"Y-yes...so weak..." The beggar smacked his lips as well and wiggled his fingertips; a trick that usually brought out the sympathy in a passer-by. But Rumpel was no ordinary passer-by; nor was he altogether very sympathetic.

"What's it to me?" Rumpel said, inching toward him, eyes on the man's bottle.

"I—I—just want something to eat..." Despite being a full three feet taller, the beggar stared at the ever-approaching gnomish man, his eyes like saucers, terrified. "or maybe..." He shifted his eyes all around. "...perchance a coin to buy a loaf?"

Rumpel thought to himself, stone-faced for several moments. The beggar squirmed, still leaning against the tree. Finally a smirk came across the gnome's face. "Perchance." he said.

THE LADY IN THE LAKE

The beggar smiled, and slowly got to his feet. He hobbled toward the small creature to shake his hand. "Oh thank you, kind one." he said, smiling with a half-set of teeth. He held out his hand, but when Rumpel did the same; his hands were equally as empty.

"Oh I've no money to **give** you." Rumpel said. "But I can..." He reached knobby hand into his jacket and pulled out his wand. He pointed the stick to a scattering of stones cast down on the roadside. "...turn these stones into rubies."

"R-rubies?" The beggar said, in disbelief. He let out a scoff and started backing away toward his tree.

"You doubt my magic?" Rumpel said, amused. The beggar only scoffed at him again. "You must not be from around here. I've just come from a man for whom I turned his straw into gold What's a few rubies to me?" He pointed his boney finger back toward the cottage, perched high on the hilltop.

"Rubies..." The man whispered. He was of two minds, on the one hand not wanting to believe such foolishness, but on the other being greedy enough to convince himself it might be true. Rumpel could read his face like an open book.

"I can turn these rocks into rubies, if that's your fancy."

"It is..." the beggar said, deciding he had nothing to lose. "Yes, it is!" He was almost salivating at the prospect. "Do it! Do it!" he said, waving the gnome on. Rumpel didn't move, however. "Well come on!"

"But what…" the small creature said, speaking very slowly and deliberately. "…will you give me…in return?" Again a thin smile crept across his tiny, bearded face.

"Anything! Anything!" The beggar said, carried away by his lust.

Rumpel was more than happy to egg his greed on. "You can have wealth."

"Yes."

"You can how power."

"Yes!"

"You could have all the women in the world!"

"Yes, anything!" The beggar said, almost jumping in place. "Anything! Anything!"

"Anything…" Rumpel repeated his words with a slight nod. "I'll hold you to that."

The beggar's smile faded as he contemplated the ramifications of making such a deal. A tear of sweat rolled down his cheek as he saw Rumpel moving toward the pile of rocks.

"Wait!" The beggar yelled. "I—I think…I've changed my mind."

"It's too late. The deal is made." Rumpel hunched over the rocks, and opened his hands. "Stand back, and watch the magic!"

A flick of his wrist, was followed by a loud

THE LADY IN THE LAKE

CRACK like a thunderbolt. A puff of blue smoke erupted from the pile of rocks, obscuring the vision of both magician and beggar. Both men coughed and waved their arms, trying in vain to wave away the choking mist.

A trio of bunnies, one white, one blue and one purple bounced out of the smoke, happy as could be, none-the-wiser that they were the product of a magical feat.

"Wha…?" Rumpel said, for once completely baffled and at a loss for words.

"Where's my money?" the old beggar demanded, unimpressed by the rabbits and in no mood to negotiate.

Quick to recover, Rumpel spun around to face him, flashing a grin that would make a used wagon salesman proud. "We agreed on rubies, yes?"

"Yeah, and thems aint that."

"Ah but rubies are red, and these bunnies are blue and purple. When you add blue and purple together you get the color red."

"No you don't!"

"How would you know, you're a beggar!"

"I was promised money!"

"Fine! You give me that bottle and I'll turn the rabbits into gold or pearls or rubies or whatever."

"My bottle? This is all I have."

"You're about to have a lot more if you just

give me that drink."

"You have your own drink right there!" the beggar pointed to Rumpel's hip-flask hanging off his belt.

"Yes but whatever you have is clearly more valuable."

"Why?"

"Because if it wasn't you'd have already drunk it by now. Now give it to me—"

"Such talent, wasted on a desire to get drunk." a bubbly voice fluttered out from behind him. Rumpel turned to see a tall man in a purple robe, spangled with stars, moons and suns, smiling at him behind a long beard that was twisted into knots.

"Who are you?" Rumpel asked.

"You can call me..." He looked left and right as if checking for eavesdroppers. His voice dropped in volume as well as he leaned forward to say: "Merlin."

"Why are we whispering?" Rumpel asked, matching Merlin's tone.

"Because I'm not supposed to use that name outside of my country."

"Oh merde, you're a guardian aren't you?"

"I am indeed." he said, smiling as he straightened his back. The smile faded after only a moment however and the wizard cleaned his throat. "But as I say, you're wasting your skills playing cons with poor beggars. And all to get

THE LADY IN THE LAKE

drunk?"

"I'm only drinking in between jobs. I got kids to feed! Besides, you can't magic water into wine, now can you?"

Before Merlin could answer with what certainly would have been a snappy retort, the beggar chimed in: "I was promised rubies!"

"My good man you'd don't need rubies, you need rupees; money made from hard work. Now up up." Merlin said, strolling by Rumpel to help the man to his feet. "If you ride on into Istanbul you'll find a man tending a bar. You tell him Merlin sent you and he'll give you a job."

"Which bar?"

"You won't be able to miss it. There's a big owl on the sign out front. The name's Hooters! Archimedes is the owner, he'll take care of you." Merlin patted the man on the back and pointed his wand at the white bunny that was still lingering nearby.

There was a *BANG* and a puff of blue smoke erupted, out of which came the rabbit, only large enough now for a grown man to ride. The wizard helped the man up and, with a slap to the animal's backside, watched him bounce away. "I'll see you soon!"

A moment of quiet reflection followed, with Merlin happily watching the beggar trot away and Rumpel awkwardly wondering how best to slip away unseen. He had been trying to vanish for the past several seconds but found the skill had suddenly left him.

"I'm blocking you." Merlin said.

"Hm?" Rumpel asked.

"From blinking out of here. I'm holding you here." Merlin said, smiling at him.

"What do you want from me? I didn't do anything to you; go back to your own country and pester them, guardian!"

"Oh if only you were the first person to tell me that. I quit worrying about that old line years ago. I have bigger fish to fry. Come on then." he said, turned on the road to follow after the beggar and bunny.

"Come on? Where? I'm not going with you."

"Sure you are. You've got little choice unless you want me to take up back up to that cottage you came from. Besides, I could use the company, someone to talk to so I don't look crazy talking to myself."

"Why don't you just not talk at all?" Rumpel snapped, annoyed as he walked alongside him.

"Because there are things to be said! It's been twenty years since the last one."

"The last…what?"

"Nevermind that; nevermind that now. The point is, people need to know what's been going on." He stopped suddenly. "You know what? Let's do this…" he flicked his wand and transformed a scurrying beetle into a pale blue donkey. Another

THE LADY IN THE LAKE

flick turned its companion into a dull grey mule with a saddle the perfect size for a man of Rumpel's small stature. "And one for you." Merlin said as he climbed on his ride.

An hour passed with little conversation between them, despite Merlin's best efforts. The road to Istanbul became more lively as they went on, with Rumpel passing up several worthwhile opportunities to con strangers out of either drinks or drinking money.

"Far be it for me to encourage bad behavior but I am curious why, if you can turn rocks into rubies don't you just buy your own drinks. Why swindle poor people out of money. Why turn straw into gold for an old farmer when you can just make gold for yourself?"

"That wasn't just any farmer." Rumpel answered with a scoff. "That was the maker of the finest Turkish wine in all this land. Besides if you got it..." he whipped out his own wand and made sparks pop out of the end. "why not use it!"

"I'm afraid you have a drinking problem, among many others."

"Yeah well I'm afraid you have a minding your own business problem. What's a wizard guardian doing outside of his own country?"

"Sibling quarrel." Merlin said. "That is to say my sibling wishes to quarrel with the world. I'm hoping to recruit some help."

"Ha!" Rumpel barked. "If you're looking for

magic-doers in the Turkish Empire you can find us, there are a few floating around. If it's help you want though, I wouldn't count on it."

"I dunno...The Turks have been inching closer to war with Rome and my sister—at least I think—is working behind the scenes with Rome. War between the two parties is inevitable, I'm afraid. So if anyone might be inclined to help I would think your people would be."

"You don't know the Turks very well then. We're not like the old Syrians."

"No...you're much more aggressive."

"We're hungry. We've been held back by old traditions for too long."

"For a crook and a magi you seem far more invested than I would have thought."

Rumpel only chuckled. "As I say, you don't know the Turks. We are a proud people."

"What can you tell me about the guardian of your land?"

"Are you serious?"

"Why wouldn't I be?" Merlin asked, unable to hide his confusion.

"What can **you** tell me about her?"

"Very little I'm afraid. I know she has never revealed herself to the rest of the guardians; I've never seen her at the annual Christmas party. I didn't even know she was a she until you just said as much."

"Well everyone here knows her. Reveres

THE LADY IN THE LAKE

her. Unlike you she doesn't leave her land. Unlike you she is committed to protecting her people."

"That's why I want to meet her. Protecting her people and stopping my sister are mutual goals."

"You really have no idea who she is?"

"No I guess not but...here I was thinking about sneaking away. But now I think I will help you find her." Rumpel said with more than a few other thoughts swimming around his mind, unsaid.

"Excellent!" Merlin replied, smiling widely at him.

*****

Istanbul was, as it had been for centuries, a bustling metropolis. But instead of the typical happy citizens, smiling and greeting tourists, passers-by, and residents alike, Merlin and Rumpel encountered mostly scowls. "Your reputation precedes you." Merlin said as they trotted through the cities wide roads.

"It's not me they dislike, wizard, it's you."

"Me? What did I do?"

"Nothing except wear that ridiculous get up." he answered, pointing at Merlin's robe and hat. "These people have learned not to trust anyone in a pointy hat like that."

"Are you implying the Turks have some deep-rooted prejudice against wizards?"

"I'm saying our people don't trust wizards and we hate guardians."

Merlin was not often completely flummoxed but he was at this moment. "But you said your guardian was revered?" Rumpel snorted in laughter. "Are you going to tell me what's so funny?"

"Not yet but remind me to tell you after you meet her. We're at your booby bar." Rumpel added, pointing to the owl-painted sign that stood atop a simple, box-shaped building in the middle of the crowded road.

"It's not—it's an owl thing! They hoot!"

They parked their donkeys along the side of the building and approached the double swinging doors of the tavern. "You're buying." Rumpel said, though Merlin's hand stopped him from entering.

"I want no funny business from you."

"Hey, you invited me to come along. You'll get whatever business I want it to be."

"Alright then…" Merlin said, pulling out his wand and winking at the small man. "Now then, you may enter."

"What'd you do?"

"Nothing…maybe a little something. Just don't try to zip out of here with some lady's purse and you'll be fine."

Merlin pushed the doors open and gestured for Rumpel to enter. An array of mostly-empty tables were scattered around on either side of the

THE LADY IN THE LAKE

doors. A T-shaped bar sat in the middle of the room, with only a few drinkers sitting on various stools an Archimedes moving back and forth, filling drinks, sliding drinks down the bar, barking orders, looking generally miserable, right at home.

"Hi welcome to Hooters!" a stilted voice said, greeting them as they stepped inside. "Would you like to try—oh it's you!"

"Ah the beggar!" Merlin said, smiling at him. "So he hired you, then?"

"Sure did. I just started an hour ago." He led them to a nearby table. "So…would you like to try our new double hooter meat pie?"

Merlin cast a quick look to Rumpel. "Alright maybe the name was a bad idea…Uh, No," he said, turning back to the now-former beggar. "Just tell Archimedes we've arrived."

"Sure." he said as he ambled away.

The bar owner arrived a few moments later, tailed by the beggar who had a trio of tall, foaming drinks in his hands. "Thanks for the help." Archimedes said, gesturing to the beggar as he placed the drinks on the table.

"You know you have to pay him." Merlin said.

"I don't even know his name. He just showed up and said you sent him, so I told him to start cleaning tables."

"What have you learned in your time here?"

Archimedes scoffed. "I learned they don't

drink like the French do."

"Nor do I." Merlin said, tapping his glass with his wand, instantly turning it into clear, cool water.

"I on the other hand..." Rumpel started but didn't bother to finish it as he downed every drop of his mug.

"What of the guardian?"

"She has a place on the Sea of Marmara. No one approaches it."

"Let me guess;" Merlin said, half-grinning, "it looks like a giant skull rising out of the water?"

"No, it's just an island. What are you talking about?"

"Oh. You sure the guardian lives there?"

"Yeah, for now. The way the locals talk, the Turks are always a week away from pressing further west. And she seems to be at the center of their conquests. They've got their eyes set on Athens right now. Although last week they were talking about Jerusalem."

"So she's active, more liberal in her thinking. Not content to 'keep the balance' as the old laws told us."

"Call it whatever you want, Merlin, that's not my expertise. All I know is she hasn't been in Istanbul forever. She's come from the deserts in the east—"

"That's just a rumor," Rumpel interjected, "no one knows where she comes from."

THE LADY IN THE LAKE

"Well she's a guardian so ultimately we know where she comes from." Merlin was quick to correct him, though Rumpel only rolled his eyes at him. "But you say she started out here in the east?"

"Yeah but like your little friend said, the common folk don't see her. Only the military people. She runs this Empire if you ask me. The Vizier is just a puppet. But that's just my impression. Your friend here may know more." Archimedes said, a little prickly, in Rumpel's direction. Merlin looked over to see if the gnome-like man wanted to add anything to the discussion.

"I don't know any more than what I've already said."

"You said you knew where to find her?"

"Did I? I think I said I wanted to be with you when **you** found her. I'm in a bit of a mess right now and meeting her, alongside you, I might add, might just get me out of it."

"Alright. Archimedes, you do you think she can be persuaded to hold off on attacking Roman territory until we can drive Morgana out of hiding?"

"Can't say. So far the Turks have only conquered land outside of Roman or Germanian jurisdiction. They made a play for some Germanian lands but backed off just as quickly. Most think it was just a test to see how Rome would react. If you ask me they're going to play the long game, swinging south to Jerusalem,

Egypt, and across the lands south of the Great Sea."

"Iberia." The old wizard said, drawing the conclusion that Archimedes was building to.

"If they take Iberia, they'll have armies on either side of Rome."

"You're talking about five, even ten years down the line." Merlin said.

Archimedes shook his head silently, however. "You're forgetting that Iberia and Rome are about to go to war themselves, and all the territory west of Egypt is easy-pickings for anyone with an army willing to conquer it…and I promise you the Turks are willing to conquer. If they made an alliance with Iberia, they could have forces there in months, not years."

Merlin thought for a moment, sipping his water. "I'm getting a refill." Rumpel said, hopping off his table and heading for the bar.

"Where'd you find him?" Archimedes asked once Rumpel was out of earshot.

"I've been following him for a few weeks now. He's got skill with a wand; thought he might be an able ally."

"He doesn't seem the ally type."

"No, but help sometimes comes in unlikely forms. Besides, better to have him in sight than out of it."

"TROLL!" a terrible, booming voice exploded around them. Merlin spun around in his

THE LADY IN THE LAKE

chair to see, standing in the entranceway, a tall, dark and utterly terrifying looking warrior of a man staring at hole into Rumpel. He was flanked a pair of almost-as-imposing swordsmen. "My master would very much like a word with you." He drew a long, curved sword as he stepped toward the frightened gnome.

Rumpel twitched in place but did not move. "What's he waiting for?" Archimedes mumbled, before yelling at him: "Just 'poof' on out of here like Merlin does."

"Don't bring me into this." Merlin said, before his conscience got the better of him. "Oh very well..." He rose from his chair. "Sorry, I blocked you from...poofing out of here, as Archimedes would say." He drew his wand. "Let's just leave until these men decide to try their business elsewhere."

"Uh, Merlin..." Rumpel said.

"Two of them." said one of the swordsmen with the large and scary man. "Get the thing."

"What thing?" Merlin asked.

They didn't answer of course, but the other swordsman pulled out a small gem from his pouch. It pulsated with a hypnotizing strobe of black and white. When he threw it on the ground it spun in place like a toy top.

"Merlin, we're going to have to fight our way out of this." Rumpel said. "Whatever you do, don't—"

"I got this." the wizard said as he pointed his wand at the trio. A loud *BANG* followed but there was no blue smoke such as what usually accompanied Merlin's spell-casting. Instead the room seemed to melt around them. Their stomachs lurched into their throats with the sensation of suddenly falling.

A moment later they landed, face-planting on the cold, stone floor of a dark and damp room filled with nothing but piles of straw and hay.

"What'd you do?" Merlin asked Rumpel as the small man pressed his palm against his face, wondering how he would weasel his way out of his newest predicament.

THE LADY IN THE LAKE

MATTHEW L. MARTIN
CHAPTER 7 : FATHER AND SONS

Eric was furious, a reaction that seemed to take even himself by surprise. His father wanted a hug and went so far as to hold his old arms out to his son for the duration of his slow approach, but Eric blew right by him, entered the church and promptly kicked over a pew.

"I got your letters." his father said. "Sorry I couldn't respond."

"Couldn't respond?!" Eric spun around to face him. "Couldn't respond?! Do you realize I've thought you were dead. I thought you'd been dead for—for nearly half my life! How hard is it to send a letter? One rook just to say you were alive!"

"I couldn't. They would have found me."

"Who?!"

THE LADY IN THE LAKE

"Templar." Sal said as he entered behind his father.

"You okay?" the old man asked him.

"Yeah he picked me up a few days ago."

"Knew he would. Good boy."

"I'm not a boy, dad, and I wasn't good when I was."

"Hi, sorry to interrupt." Marcella said, entering after Sal and taking a spot next to Eric.

"Morné." the old man said, extending a hand to the lady. "You with him."

"Yeah we all are. There's a whole wagonfull back there."

"You got kids?" Morné asked, perking up.

"No, not like that. Sorry."

"I've been trying to get this one to find someone to make me some grandbabies with." he said, tugging at Sal's arm. "How can a man be almost eighty and not have any grandkids?!" He flashed a smile at Eric who did not reciprocate. "How can he be almost fifty and not have any kids!? What've you been doing with your time, son?"

"What's going on here, dad?"

"Yeah, we have a lot of questions."

"Alright come in and sit down, I'll tell you everything I can. You can tell the rest of your group to come too if you want."

*****

MATTHEW L. MARTIN

They sat scattered around a large fellowship room in the back of the church, with Eric, Marcella, Morné and Sal occupying one table. "It started years ago. Templar raids all long the French/Roman border."

"What were you doing this far from home?"

"I've been here since not long after you joined the army."

"I didn't join, remember. They drafted me out of prison."

"Yes well, all the same. You went off to war and I decided to get back into the church. Only around that time a new Pope was appointed and tensions between Rome and France picked up. There was talk of Rome withdrawing all priests from France and other talk of King Leon—rest his soul—starting his own church and conscripting French priests to the new religious order. I left Dole because the people were bit too eager to follow whatever Leon wanted. Grenoble is a little more liberal and a little less crazy."

"And then the Templar came." Sal said, prodding his father on.

"Wait, where did **you** come from?" Eric asked, not minding his lack of tact.

"He came…around that time. My transition back to the ministry was a slow process. There were mistakes made…the consequences of which I do not regret." he added quickly, patting his son on the arm.

THE LADY IN THE LAKE

"And where's your mother?" Eric asked. It was the second time he'd directed a question to Sal and for the second time it was their father who spoke for him.

"She's gone. Once I told her my plans to be a priest again she left and left the boy behind."

"I was abandoned too!" Jay shouted from the table behind them. Eric turned back, unsurprised to see the whole rest of his group was hanging on every word Morné was saying. Jay slunk down a bit in his chair. "My family are travelling performers. Trick and games and acrobatics and such. They have all girls and I was a boy so they…just left."

"This is some team you've brought me." Morné said returning awkwardly to their conversation. "I suppose they're good at what they do."

"Why are we here?" Eric asked flatly.

"I heard you were back in France and I wanted to see you." Eric only shook his head, not buying the story for a moment. "Alright, we **are** in a bit of trouble. Grenoble's mayor asked if I could help and I'd heard for a several years now about your exploits. I almost hired you three years ago but I chickened out."

"Why did you send that man to our bar?" Marcella asked. "Why not just send Sal or send a letter."

"Why not send a letter twenty-five years

ago!" Eric added with a little more pepper than Marcella had.

"I told you, the Templar have been chasing me."

"No. Not that long ago. Why didn't you write when I first sent word I was in England?"

"They weren't allowing any communication to reach England for years after you and that King of yours landed. By the time I could send a rook, I was here and Sal was born and the Templar began making raids across the border. There was too much going on."

"Too much to let your son know you were okay?"

"Well I wasn't okay. I spent two years in a Roman prison and when I got out I returned here and picked up where I left off."

"They arrested you for…preaching?" Marcella asked.

"For organizing a resistance." Sal said.

"You're being grandiose. He's being grandiose."

"What are you doing? What are you resisting?"

"The Templar have been trying to burn Grenoble to the ground for years now. The French government is unwilling to directly engage them. So we take matters into our own hands. It's not like the full Roman army or anything. It's only ever just a handful of them, riding in with torches

THE LADY IN THE LAKE

and a bad attitude."

"Last time it was twenty."

"Which was more than enough."

"How many do you command?"

"Well we had about one-hundred able bodied men willing to fight."

"Had?"

"Those twenty Templar were very good with a crossbow." Morné said.

"There's no one left." Sal said.

"What do you want us to do?"

"What do you think? We want you to be the heroes. When the Templar come back, they're going to be expecting a town full of scared women and old men. They know there's no one left to defend us. You'll get the jump on them and… you know, save the day or whatever."

"I think it's a win-win." Jay said, now standing behind Eric. "They get some help, we get the rest of the money promised us, you get to reconnect with your dad—"

"Go sit down." Eric said sharply.

"Oh yeah, there's no more money." Sal said. "O'Mare gave you all we had in the coffers."

"It's alright; they're not doing this for money." Morné assured his second son.

"We're not?" Eric asked.

"Of course we're not." Marcella was quick to say.

"So that's it then, you're hired?" Morné

asked, holding his open hand out for Eric to shake.

"It's not a hire if there's no money..." Eric said, hesitating. "I have a lot more questions....but yes we'll help you." he sighed, reaching a hand toward his dad, who took his and shook it with the vigor of a man half his age.

"Great. We have rooms for you to sleep in upstairs. The Templar will be here next full moon."

"That's two days away!" Eric said.

"Yes, and I have all the confidence in you!" Morné said, rising from the table.

"Two days is Sunday." Marcella said, suddenly realizing it.

"That doesn't matter." Sal said, bitterly. "No one comes to worship here anyway."

*****

There were three rooms to spare, and the six of them paired up and separated for the night, each thinking about what strategy they would employ to defeat a band of Templar with twenty-to-six odds against them.

Eric's door knocked a few minutes after he and Marcella settled in. He opened it to see Sal standing sheepishly on the other side. "I wanted to apologize."

"For lying to me or for something else?"

"I couldn't exactly say 'hey I'm your half-brother, nice to meet you, dad's waiting...' I was told not to say anything until we got here."

THE LADY IN THE LAKE

Eric stepped aside to let him enter. He didn't offer the young man a chair, however but instead sat down on the bed and looked up at him, waiting for him to ask to sit down. He never did. "So. You said sorry. What else you have to say?"

"Stop it Eric, this is your brother." Marcella said before turning to him. "Sit, please. I was curious why you said no one comes to worship here."

"Dad is not...well liked among the people. He stirred up the fighting men against the Templar and now that they're either dead or too injured to fight there's a lot of resentment against him."

"Well do they want their town burned to the ground?!"

"I think if you asked a single person that, he'd say no. But a person is rational. **People** are dumb. And it's easier to cast blame than take matters into your own hands."

"What about you?" Eric asked. "Where were you the last time the Templar came to town?"

"On my way with O'Mare to find you. We heard your group liked to hang out at that bar."

"Not anymore I guess."

"Why not anymore?" Marcella asked. "It's not the first time we've caused a bar fight. Raph'll be fine."

"Nah, there's too much heat on us now. We've never killed a handful of Roman citizens. As long as France and Rome have their non-agreement agreement, we're going to be hunted."

"I told you not to kill him." Marcella said, unable to restrain herself.

"I left one alive. The Inquisitor."

"You what?!" Sal said, jumping off the bed. "You fought an Inquisitor?"

"Yeah just before we left. Wasn't much of a fight. They let the white robes do the dirty work for them."

"When did this happen?" Marcella asked.

"In between the time we killed the Templar in the bar and when we stole their carriage. I saw him dive into one of the rent houses to hide and I went after him. You were smoothing things over with Raph."

"What'd you do?"

"I went in and…let some aggression out. But I didn't kill him."

"Why not, you killed everyone else?" Sal said, eyes wide with panic.

"He never even attacked me. Just let me wail on him. It was weird. It was like he was enjoying it, watching me scream at him and punch him over and over. I decided I'd hurt him enough that killing him would just be a relief. I left him to suffer."

"You left him to identify you." Sal said. "He will eventually get word back to Rome."

"He knew who I was." Eric shrugged. "He knew I was the Templar hunter. We probably

THE LADY IN THE LAKE

crossed paths before. It doesn't matter; we're a long way from there now."

"It does matter. They'll know we're here." Sal said, now pacing the room.

"Calm down. How can they know?"

"They have spies everywhere. It's not just Templar and Inquisitors. They have disciples in black, Roman citizens secretly living in the Kingdoms all over the Old Lands, sending reports. They are connected all the way up to Pope Benedictus."

"You make it sound a lot worse than it is." Eric said, unfazed. "Rome is bad, I hear you. But they're just an Empire like France or England."

"Oh? Does England have plans to overthrow governments and establish a global Kingdom?"

"From what I hear, England doesn't even have plans to throw a Christmas party this year. They're not the best-run country anymore." Eric replied, unable to contain a note of bitterness.

"Well Rome is. They are the best-run country, and their ambitions are big. While you've been hopping around France, breaking into manors and picking pockets—"

"Hey!"

"—We've been over here pushing against the tide!"

"Oh please." Eric stood up, towering over the younger, smaller Sal. "One little town under a mountain, fights off a few arsonists and you think you're saving the world."

"Well what have **you** been doing to save the world?"

"I haven't been, but I'm not the one bragging about it."

"I'm not bragging!"

"Well what are you doing then?!"

"Something! Which is more than you've been doing. I'm not bragging…I'm blaming you for making my life a lot harder now!"

"This isn't about some Inquisitor who may or may not know where we are."

"He does."

"This is about me and my dad and our problems that go back long before you were even born."

"Yeah…you're not far off." Sal snapped. "You left, I didn't. You ran off—"

"I was drafted!"

"You ran off to England. I didn't leave. I stuck by his side, helped him make something of his life. So yeah, this is about you and him and whatever problems there were between you. But the only reason you're here is because he knew you'd help. That's it. You're not here to reconcile or reconnect or move back home to take care of 'old dad;' that's my job. You're here to do this job; you take out those Templar, however many there are—"

"Twenty, you already said."

THE LADY IN THE LAKE

"It was twenty before you left that Inquisitor alive."

"Why am I getting grief for **not** killing someone!?"

"It's going to be a lot more of them when they come."

"Well…we'll think of something."

"You do that. I will too." Sal said, spinning around for the door.

"What does that mean?"

"It means what I said. I'll think of my own plan." And with that, he slammed the door behind him.

"How'd that go? Okay?" he asked Marcella after a quiet moment passed. She had no answer, except to rest her face in her hand. "It'll be fine. We'll think of something; we always do."

MATTHEW L. MARTIN
CHAPTER 8 : FALLEN KINGDOM

Typically, when a King rides to war, the people flock to the streets to see his passing procession, waving at him as the army rides by, perhaps throwing flowers at his feet or serenading him with sonnets of impending victory. When Mordred and his army marched north to quell the rebellion of the Scottish Lords, the streets were bare and the people hidden.

"No one here seems concerned about the threat in the Scottish lands." Mordred said as they marched through Leeds. "We're only a few days from York, too."

THE LADY IN THE LAKE

"I'm sure they're plenty worried your grace." Sir Richard said, riding beside him.

"If they were you'd think they'd be outside their homes cheering us on."

"Hatred trumps worry, your grace." Sir Hanbury said, riding behind him, turning to Sir Terance to share the smirk with him.

"The King is not hated." Sir Richard said briskly. "The times are hard and the people have little to cheer. They support his grace's army as we march north. Only a weakling needs flowers and song when he rides for war."

"And what do you need, Sir Richard?" Hanbury hissed. "What goodie was offered to you to get you out of Camelot for a change?"

"What are you implying, Sir Hanbury?" Mordred asked, once again having failed to catch the sarcasm.

"The good Knight only means Sir Richard is usually one to plot from a desk, not ride to battle." Sir Terance said. He might've said more but Richard had turned his steed to stop the Knight from advancing, a murderous look flashed across his face. Terance's thin face remained frozen but his large red mustache twitched with the rhythm of his heartbeat. He was nervous and it was obvious.

"You talk too much." Richard said between gritted teeth.

"Enough." Mordred said. The army was

behind them, waiting for the signal to continue marching, ripples of murmurs moving through their ranks. "It is almost sunset, we should make camp at plan our strategy for dealing with the Scots, not quibble amongst ourselves."

"It is only 5:30 by the look of it...plenty of daylight left to march under." Sir George said, trotting up to join the fun.

"If we were going to make camp we should have made it in Leeds. We were just there." Sir Maris whined.

"Stop your complaining and organize the camp." Richard snapped at him. Maris slunked away, grumbling as he did so.

"His grace has the finest, bravest and most loyalist army I've ever seen." Hanbury said, his tone dripping in sarcasm that Mordred only caught by gauging the reaction of Sir Richard.

"Pitch my tent and organize the Table to convene as soon as we can." the King said before turning his horse away from their sneering smiles of feigned respect.

*****

"Far be it for me to tell you how to manage your Roundtable—" Sir Richard began.

"No, please. I certainly need the help." Mordred replied. They were sitting alone in his tent that evening, waiting for the rest of his advisers to join them. As usual, they were late.

THE LADY IN THE LAKE

"It's just, they do not respect you."

"Of course they don't; even I can tell that."

"If you would be a little more…assertive, perhaps. Find a course of action and demand they comply."

"That's not really…I'm much better at hearing their suggestions and just picking one."

"Yes and while you hear their suggestions they argue amongst themselves and mock you for your own indecisions. These are Knights, older perhaps but soldiers all the same. They need structure and leadership."

The tent flap whipped open and a procession of Roundtable members entered in a row, ending the conversation. One by one they sat around the circular table, each looking to Sir Richard—not Mordred—to call the meeting to order. To their surprise, the King cleared his throat and stood. "Even with the Irish supporting the Scots, we still have superior numbers. We will send over an army of Welshmen to the Island and seize it in the name of England. The Irish that are here will either let their Kingdom burn or they will surrender, crippling the Scots before—"

"It would take too long to organize such a movement." Sir George said dismissively. Mordred immediately returned to his chair. "This war will be finished before they even land on Ire's Island."

"Sir Oxlef would not be happy for us to send

fellow Welshmen to battle without his leading them. Not to mention the fact that he has five-thousand of his best Welshmen in York right now." Sir Grummore said. "The better course of action is to hold the Scots and Irishmen in the north country, reinforce York and wait."

"Wait?" Mordred said, now fully engaged in the debate as though he was just another advisor. "Wait for what?"

"For…your brother." Grummore replied, timidly.

"My brother? What about him?"

"I sent a rook when we made camp, informing—" His words were cut short by a sudden outburst of chatter, with some seizing on the development to toss out their own strategies and others chiding the Knight for overstepping his bounds.

"That was not your place!" Sir Richard shouted, his voice piercing through the crosstalk.

"It had to be done!" Grummore snapped back at him, defensively. "This is war and we need every advantage."

"That was not your decision to make!"

"Someone had to do it!"

"Yes, the King!" Richard was standing now, fists clenched.

"I agree." Grummore said, rising up as well. "The King should have made that decision…but the King did not make it. So I made it."

THE LADY IN THE LAKE

"The King's brother—" Richard began

"is a weapon!" Grummore interjected.

"No." Mordred said. "Freak though he may be, he is life and life is sacred." Those were the words of his mother. He could repeat them if not understand them. "My brother will remain safe at Camelot. We will defeat this rebellion without him."

"Your grace—" Sir Terance said, once more feigning deference."

"I'm sure what you're about to say will be a very eloquent statement in support of Sir Grummore, but I'm not interested in hearing it, thank you." Mordred rose as Richard and Grummore slowly returned to their seats. "We will continue to York and we will stall the Scottish forces, not to summon my brother but to give the Welsh time to sail to Ire's Island. When the island is taken we will parlay with the Irish as Sir Maris previously suggested." Mordred look toward Maris, forcing himself to make eye contact with him long enough to see him nodding in approval.

"I think it's an excellent idea." Sir Hanbury said, startling everyone.

"You do?" Sir Richard replied.

"Certainly. They are distracted in the North, we swoop in under their noses and take control of their home. They will have no choice but to parlay."

"Excellent. That's the plan then." Mordred

said.

"I'll send a rook to Bridgend immediately." Hanbury said.

"Alright...." Mordred looked around the room awkwardly. He usually left it to Richard to call the meeting to a close. "Dis—uh, dismissed?" He exhaled as everyone filed out of his tent, leaving him alone to rest and sigh in relief that he might yet avoid having to do any personal fighting.

*****

Two days later, the English army reached York, relieved for a moment to find a sizeable number of forces waiting for them. Sir Oxlef rode out to meet Mordred as they approached. "Your grace, the Scot and Irish forces number thirty-thousand. Sir Dondal is meeting with their representative now, though I do not expect them to withdraw.

"Where are the rebel forces now?" Sir Richard asked.

"Darlington."

"Darlington?! They're in England? Last we heard they were holding place in Fallstone."

"They were as of a week ago, but they pressed south and took the Peace Road to Darlington. The city fell with little incident."

"Well that's good at least." Mordred liked the sound of "little incident."

THE LADY IN THE LAKE

"It is not, your grace. Many other towns along the Peace Road were plundered and burned. Darlington's surrender was more about avoiding **more** needless death. The Irish have emboldened the Scots in more ways than one." Oxlef said. "They have greater numbers now than ever before but they're also far more aggressive and unwilling to negotiate. We think they killed the city chancellor."

"Why would they do that? Wouldn't he have made a better hostage?" Mordred asked.

"Yes he would, but as I say, the Irish…"

"Yes…well we are a good two weeks away from doing anything—" Mordred began, only to be cut off by Sir White.

"Your grace, they have sacked an English city and killed an English official. We can not wait two weeks to respond!"

"I don't understand," Oxlef said, looking from White to Mordred, "two weeks until what?"

"Come Sir Oxlef, I will fill you in." Sir Hanbury said gleefully. Oxlef trotted to the Knight and they broke ranks to converse in private.

"Your grace, we can not wait for the Welsh invasion." White reiterated.

"I'm afraid I must agree." Sir Richard said. "If the Irish are as blood-thirsty as has been said, they will attack long before that, catching us flat-footed."

"Perhaps I can…" Mordred started but lost

the nerve to finish his thought.

"What? Negotiate with the rebels yourself?" Sir Terance said with a sneer. Sir Richard bit his tongue but looked to Mordred to stand up for himself.

Mordred stiffened his back. "Prepare our forces to march. We're going to Darlington. Now."

"Now?" Terance said. "We've only just arrived. We should wait till morn—"

"No waiting." Mordred said, unable to hide his childish bitterness. "As you all have said, my plan was no good, so fine. You want to meet them face to face, let's go." He turned to the bannerman sitting silently to his left. "Blow the horn; we're going."

*****

"Oxlef was mistaken on two counts." Sir Richard said, riding back to the King after meeting with a scout. "The combined Scottish and Irish army number nearly forty-thousand, almost matching our number that rides to meet them."

"Two counts?" Mordred asked.

"They have left Darlington and will meet us in Farlington by mid-day."

"Have we heard from Sir Dondal?" Mordred asked.

"Scout says he saw the Lord's horse but she was being ridden by Lord Fenial."

"That's not a good omen." Sir Maris

THE LADY IN THE LAKE

mumbled from behind the King.

"Were we expecting Lord Fenial to lead the army?" Mordred asked.

Richard only shrugged. "It's his rebellion. I don't see why he wouldn't."

"When we meet, I will go and negotiate."

Richard hesitated and clearly wanted to talk Mordred out of it, but he held his peace and merely nodded. A persistent overcast followed them all the way from Camelot but it never rained on them. Storms broke out in towns and cities after they left but no once did the English army meet the English weather. Then, as the noon sun peaked overhead and the Scot/Irish army approached, the clouds opened and a downpour began, pelting all sides with fat drops of rain from the sky.

Unfazed, Mordred left the vanguard and rode the center between the two forces. Lord Fenial did the same, meeting him in the middle. The Scot was lean and muscular, with a head full of brown hair and eyes as wild as a mad man. His face was painted blue and green—a show of solidarity between the Scots and the Irish—though whatever effect he was hoping for was mitigated by the persistent deluge from above.

"Your glace." Fenial said, spitting droplets of blue and green as he spoke with half-way intelligible English.

"Lord Fenial."

"**King** Fenial, now."

"King?"

"King of the Scots and the Ilish."

"King of both? What do the Irish think of that?"

"They'll come a'lound to it after your army's been defeated."

Mordred ignored that. "I come with terms."

"Do you? So do I."

"You and your rebellion against the English crown must end. Your army will return to their homes in the North, the Irish to their island and you will answer for your crimes at Camelot." Mordred waited for a reply but none came. He rehearsed the speech a dozen times the night before and each time imagined all the different things that might be said in response.

He was ready with a response to the response but no response came. So he continued, a little shaken and a little more timidly than before. "None of your people will be arrested or brought to court. Only you will answer for the rebellion."

Fenial edged his horse—Dondal's horse—closer to Mordred's. The beast snorted in the face of the English King's horse, causing it to sneeze. Modred's attention drifted down to the animal, away from Fenial who was continuing to stare silently at him. "So…do you agree?" Mordred asked finally asked.

"…"

"Say something already!"

THE LADY IN THE LAKE

"Here are my terms. Your army can go, plovided they lay down they'll weapons and surrender all future claim to all the lands north of York. That's now the English border, York."

"Obviously we'll have to negotiate that point—"

"I'm not finished." Fenial said. "I've no interest in take you as a prisoner of my Kingdom but I do demand you tell the tluth to all the people you've lied to over the years, m'self included."

Mordred stared dumbfounded at him, which probably made him seem guiltier by the second. Finally he spoke, without any command or force behind his words, a meek and meager "I don't know what that means."

"You are no lightful King of England. I knew Arthur. I served in his Roundtable." He put a finger in Mordred's face. "And you are as much his son as I am."

A rush of hate washed over Mordred. From some deep, unknown place it consumed him, filling his every thought and impulse with a desire to kill. *The man is a liar*, he told himself, *a wannabe usurper who now tries to discredit my legitimacy as King*. His fingers wrapped around his sword and he drew his blade to take off the Scotsman's head. He swung his arm, gripping the handle tight, fully aware that to run sharpened steel through a man's flesh and bone was no easy feat.

But he slipped, lost his balance and fell of his horse.

Fenial roared with laughter, turned his horse around and trotted back to his army, leaving the King of England sitting stupidly in the muck and mud. Sir Richard was at his side only moments later, helping him up and back on his horse. "I take it they did not surrender?" he said to the King.

Mordred did not speak until he had returned to the vanguard of his army. All eyes were on him, waiting for his speech, his rallying cry, something vocal and raucous to stir his fighters into a frenzy. He looked behind him, squinting through the rain to see Fenial racing his horse back and forth in front of his army, arms gesturing alongside what seemed to be a rip-roaring speech. He turned back to his own army, opened his mouth to speak…and threw up.

His ears were ringing but the muffled sound of Sir Richard shouting men into position gave him a slight bit of comfort. *They don't need me*, he said with relief. *I can just hang back and trust in our superior forces.*

The English had a ten-thousand man advantage and used it to great effect, spreading out in a line and forcing the Scots to thin themselves out in the middle to match them. Sir Richard took the right flank, while Sir Maris handled the left. Sirs Oxlef, Hanbury and Terance

THE LADY IN THE LAKE

took position over the rearguard, where some five thousand Welshmen were holding position, waiting to attack.

The battle began with Richard's army converging against the Irish forces on the right flank. The Irish were less-experienced and Richard insisted on personally leading the engagement against them, hoping to break them quickly and crash into the middle of the line, making for a quick end to the conflict.

Melee fighting ensued, ad though the initial English charge did manage to drive the enemy back, the rain-soaked terrain proved to be an equalizer for the smaller Irish numbers. Loses piled up on both sides and the quick end that Richard sought for soon pulled out of reach. Meanwhile the remaining Scot/Irish troops held position, with none breaking ranks to aid their fellows.

"Why don't they engage?" Mordred asked, forgetting that Sir Richard was not alongside him. The bannerman to his left turned to him, surprised to be spoken to by the King.

"They, uh...appear to be waiting for the signal to do so, your grace."

"Well let's not follow their timetable..." Mordred said, finding Sir Maris at the front of the left flank. "Engage!" he shouted but Sir Maris did not seem to hear him. "I said charge!" he shouted, and all at once the army behind him rushed ahead, charging at what they thought was his command, toward the center of the battlefield.

The Scot/Irish middle charged also, engaging in the suddenly-swampy field, as rain and blood splattered all around. Behind the King, five-thousand Welsh reserves held the rearguard, waiting for the call to move. Watching the battle, Mordred could tell that his side seemed to be holding onto the upper hand.

The reckless Irish were finally being routed by Richard's troops, while Maris' fighters were pushing into the middle, pinning Fenial and the center of his forces into a pincer. *I think we're winning. I think we're going to win.* He looked back to his Welsh cavalry and waved them forward, to trample the Scottish middle and secure the victory.

The Welshmen advanced, thundering their horses past Mordred, swords drawn. They sliced and stabbed and gutted the English as they rode, leaving a trail of bodies in their wake. It was chaos, pandemonium, a flurry of bloodshed and a cacophony of pained cries and shouts of rage that Mordred at first was unable to distinguish.

And then, with a terrible realization, he knew: The Welsh had turned coat; they were attacking their own. Oxlef had betrayed him. He looked to his right to see Hanbury sitting a'horse right next to him, blade drawn and eyes full of malice. Mordred gripped his sword but there not enough time to react; Mordred had little skill to

THE LADY IN THE LAKE

react appropriately anyway. He was stabbed in the side, just below his ribcage and once again fell off his horse, sinking into the softened ground, watching as the Welsh, Irish and Scottish routed the English and secured a victory for King Fenial.

Lord Hanbury hopped off his steed and stood over the fallen Mordred, looming over him with a sleazy grin on his face. "What a disappointment you've turned out to be. And we all had such hopes for you. You seemed like you had a real killer instinct as a boy, always running around plucking wings off pigeons and stabbing horses in the stalls. You were such a little monster, but you grew into such a pathetic King."

"Ill-made." Mordred replied. His body was cold except for the opening in his side which burned as if over an open flame.

"Yes, ill-made and ill-advised. You trusted the wrong counselors. I could have been your best advisor but instead you shut me out...or you let Richard shut me out, either way. He only wanted your mother anyway. Me, I couldn't care less about her; I just wanted your ear." Hanbury looked back to find Fenial, trotting happily along the battlefield, shouting words of encouragement to his trifecta of warriors. He didn't even notice that Mordred was still clutching his sword.

"Oxlef..." Mordred muttered.

Hanbury shrugged. "Didn't take much convincing. All I had to do was promise—"

But what he promised was left unsaid. With whatever strength he had in his depleting body, Mordred quickly swung his sword forward and pushed it in, running it through Hanbury's stomach and out the other side. The Lord Knight fell to the ground, bleeding out next to him with a look of shock and disappointment frozen onto his face.

Scot and Irish soldiers converged on their location and Mordred's sword and hand flopped back to the ground as his eyes darkened. "England surrenders." he muttered as they scooped up his limp body and carried it away…

THE LADY IN THE LAKE

MATTHEW L. MARTIN
CHAPTER 9 : REVELATION

The work had been done, the plan put in place; Eric's team was scattered around the town square, in the heart of Grenoble, ready to make their move. According to Morné, the Templar and Inquisitor would be passing through to speak to the town's magistrate at high noon outside the courthouse. If the magistrate failed to appear, the Inquisitor would deem he—and by extension, all of Grenoble—impure in the sight of God and worthy of death.

"Blah blah blah, something like that, right?" Eric said, checking his facts with his dad before taking his position.

"Yes, something like that. They're serious

THE LADY IN THE LAKE

about the 'worthy of death' stuff though; they killed the last magistrate for opposing them. That's when we decided to take action."

"Oh I know they're serious. I've tangled with them before."

"That's why we called you…and…to see you again." Morné added hastily.

"Right."

"So where should I be?"

"Back at the church; you don't need to be in the middle of this."

"No I want to help—"

"Dad—"

"Hey, **I've** been tangling with these guys too, you know."

"You wanted our help, so let us help." Eric turned away from his father, to face the front of the tavern that was to be his spot to wait at before the plan was to commence. His dad did not take the hint that the conversation was ended, however.

"I called you to finish the job. I set them up, you knock them down. I'm not some old man who can't do anything."

"That's **literally** what you are, dad. You lost your…army" (he said, with a hint of derision) "and now you need my team to take over. So let us take over."

"Take o—man you may be grown but you don't come to my town and talk to me like this. This is my plan. I'm in charge."

"You're in charge?!" Eric said, blood pressure rising.

"I'm in charge."

"Okay…" Eric nodded while his mind raced to come up with just the right comeback. Before he could, however:

"Where's Sal? He'll back me up."

"Oh I'm sure he will." They both looked left and right but couldn't find Sal. "He's supposed to be on the second floor balcony of the Inn." Eric said, pointing to the building across from the tavern. "Jay!" he shouted.

Jay popped out of an empty barrel that had been inconspicuously perched just off the road that passed through the square. The long hooped rope he was holding came untied as he leapt out onto the road. Quickly he fumbled to redo the knot. "Got it!" he shouted.

"Jay, not yet; where's Sal?"

"I haven't seen him since breakfast." The young boy said, looking around. "I've been in the thing for an hour. It's really stuffy in there."

"What's going on?" Marcella asked, sliding down a rope from the roof of the tavern.

"We can't find Sal." Morné said.

"No, we—it's fine." Eric said, frustrated. "He's probably just at the wrong Inn or something." He spotted Petro moseying over from the entrance of the Inn, converging on Eric with an inquisitive look. "Everyone get back to your spots;

THE LADY IN THE LAKE

they'll be here soon."

"Templar!" Fortigo shouted, sticking his head out of pile of loose straw and hay; his vantage point gave him a line of sight that looked down on the winding road leading up to the town.

"Yes Fortigo. We have about an hour before—"

"No, now! I see two carriages and five horsemen. Inquisitor too!"

"They're early." Eric cursed. "Back to the church;" he said to Morné, "if Sal is there tell him to get to his spot; he can sneak in through the Inn's back door."

"If he's not there—" his dad started to reply.

"If he's not there, you sit tight and let us do our job. We've got it planned out."

"I should take his spot on the balcony!"

"You are not jumping two stories down onto a horse; go!"

Morné shuffled away, leaving Eric and Marcella to race back into the tavern. Marcella ran past him toward the stairway that led to the second floor. Eric took his place just inside the door, leaning over to peek out the window, waiting for the moment to strike. All the work was done; the plan was solid. If everyone played their part right, they could have the Inquisitor taken without any—

"Eric." Marcella said.

"Get upstairs, hurry!" he whispered,

184

keeping his eyes out the window. He could see down the road as the caravan approached. Another minute and they'd be right where he wanted them—

"Eric." Sal said.

"Wha—" He turned around to see Marcella, standing stiff, arms straight at her sides, palms open. An arm was draped across her collarbone, the hand at the end of which was squeezing her shoulder. Another hand was clinched into a fist, a dagger blade sticking out of it, pressed tight against her throat. His eyes peeled away from hers, to the dark irises of Sal.

"Take off your belt." Sal said calmly. Eric obliged, dropping it and his forest green scabbard-and-sword to the floor with a thud. "The dagger on your hip." was the next command and a moment later it too was slid free from its holster and dropped to the ground, stabbing the wood floor and standing erect next to Eric's right foot. "Anything else?"

"No, that's it." Eric said.

"What do you think?" Sal asked, giving Marcella a little squeeze. She winced but did not cry out. "Is that all he's got?"

"Yes." she answered through gritted teeth.

"Alright, then let's go outside."

Eric stepped out of the Tavern, backing down the steps onto the main street behind him. His gaze was locked onto Marcella, but in the corner of his eye he could see the horsemen slowly trotting toward him, with no indication that they were at all surprised to see him.

"How long have you been planning this? From the beginning?"

"Ya see; I knew you'd say something like that. I knew you'd jump right to thinking I was a traitor from the beginning. No. Don't flatter yourself. I didn't go to all this trouble just for you. This isn't even about you, which I'm sure you don't believe."

"Yeah, I don't. If you wanted to turn our dad over you'd have done it before I showed up—"

"I'm not turning my dad over to them." Sal said, jerking his head in the direction of the horses and carriages that had now come to a halt with the riders watching the argument with, no doubt, great amusement. "I did this to **save** my dad." A look of realization crept over Eric's face, which Sal noticed immediately. "There it is." he said. "My dad is worth nothing to them, but he's worth everything to me. You? You're worth a lot to them..." He left the last line of that statement go unsaid, but the point was made all the same.

"You're a fool if you think they'll let him live. They'll probably kill you too."

Sal just shook his head as Eric seethed at his half-brother's obvious arrogance. "I cut a deal."

"You made a deal with the Devil, that's

what you did. It's not going to go how you think it will."

"Enough talk." a third voice shouted, from Eric's left. A figure in striped shades of red dismounted and stared at them, his expression indecipherable behind his tall, pointed mask. "Is this him?" he said, looking at Sal but gesturing at Eric. His accent was thick, a low and rumbling timbre that slipped out from between barely-moving lips.

"Yes."

The Inquisitor turned his body toward Eric, who kept his shoulders square and facing Marcella and Sal. "There was a man born in Seville, about ninety years ago. Ninety years ago in just a few weeks in fact. His name was Valesco, do you know it?"

"No." Eric said.

"He was my father. He served as a priest in southern Iberia for years and years before becoming an Inquisitor to the Holy Father."

"I thought you people weren't allowed to breed." Eric spat.

"That's quite the hypocritical statement, considering your own father and his relationship with the cloth." For a moment the scene remained quiet, then the Inquisitor casually started pulling off his red gloves. "You set his church house on fire. The one in Turin, do you remember? It was the headquarters for the Templar in that region."

THE LADY IN THE LAKE

Eric did not respond. In his mind he was running through all various Templar and Inquisitors he'd killed, and all the headquarters he'd burned down. He did remember more than a few visits to Rome, and to the northern country near Turin. "I expect you have long forgotten that day." the Inquisitor said.

"Just another Saturday." Eric replied coldly.

"Yes. Well today is Thursday and it will be a day I will **not** forget."

"Alright." Sal said. "Take him and go, or kill him here if you have to, but leave this town alone."

The Inquisitor inhaled a slow, deliberate breath. "I don't know…"

"No, don't do that." Sal said. "We had a deal. You get your man and we get peace."

"Peace…This whole town stands in rebellion to God and to God's appointed King on earth, the Holy Father Pope Benedictus. There can be no peace where there is rebellion."

"I gave you Eric!"

"Child, we would have gotten him anyway, and the rest of his little friends." He turned his head back to the Templar who, to that point, had remained stationary on their horses. At the Inquisitor's signal they dismounted, drawing swords and slowly approaching their master.

"Wait!" Sal shouted. "They have a man inside the Inn, and another in the barrel. There's another in the haystack."

"You stupid—!" Eric cursed him. "They are still going to kill you!"

Sal looked from Eric to the Inquisitor, very much like a confused young man who hadn't realized until that exact moment just what a terrible mess he'd gotten into.

*****

The cell door opened and Morné was thrown inside with Eric. He had a swollen cheek below his left eye and a cut above it. "I was worried about you." he said as Eric picked him up off the cold stone floor.

"You're the one who needs worrying. I thought you were dead."

"Not yet." he said, laughing with a wheeze despite the circumstances. "They didn't tell me much but I can guess what went down."

"Yeah."

"You should have let me take the balcony. You needed that one more man for the plan to work."

"You couldn't have done anything. By the time we stepped outside they were on top of us…" Eric answered robotically, having only half-heard what his father said. "Wait, what?"

"Your plan was good but without Sal you were a man short…has he turned up?"

"Sal?"

"If not he'll be along soon. Sharp kid that

THE LADY IN THE LAKE

one. Might be planning a break-out. Dunno why they didn't just kill us on the spot, though."

"Sal **is** around, dad. He turned us over to them." Eric expected his father to protest, to deny the possibility, maybe even scold him for saying something like that. But instead he remained still and quiet, but for his eyes moving left and right, piecing the obvious truth together. Finally he sighed and his face slacked. He seemed to age ten years in that one instant.

"Foolish boy." Morné mumbled, but before Eric could offer a word of agreement, his dad added: "Just like you were."

"No." Eric said. "I was foolish, yes, but I would never do what he did."

"What did he do? Turn you over to the Romans? It's about as bad as stealing from the church treasury and skipping town."

"I paid for my crimes." Eric said tersely.

"And he'll pay for his. You don't like him because you feel guilty."

"I—what? No. I don't like him because he's ignorant and arrogant and because **he** doesn't like **me** because I was your first born."

"Don't turn this into that."

"I didn't; he did."

"Enough." Morné pushed him off and slowly made his way to the rock slab in the corner of the cell to sit down. "I don't need this arguing. I didn't bring you here for that."

"That's right, you brought me here to solve a problem. I was about to. I was three minutes away from doing it. Then your son blew it up in my face."

"I told you I don't want to hear about that. He made a mistake and he'll have to live with the consequences."

"They're going to kill you, dad!"

"Like I said; he'll have to live with that. I'm ready to die. Are you?"

"No!" Eric shouted, prompting a Templar to bang the pommel of his sword on the cell bar. Morné noticed the guard for the first time, a faint smile crept on his face but it was gone just as quickly as Eric plopped down next to him. "I've never been ready. I watched my best friend die in my arms and he looked so at peace. I was terrified…to terrified to join him. I would rather have been the one survivor, alone and afraid than die with the rest of them. I was a Knight, dad."

"I know. A good one too I heard, served two Kings and two countries. Not many can say that."

"I'm sorry I did that."

"Did what?"

"Stole the money."

"Oh it was…what, thirty years ago? You were a kid; kid's are stupid."

"I was twenty. Old enough to know better."

"No you were twenty, old enough to still be stupid…just like Sal."

THE LADY IN THE LAKE

The Templar Knight guarding the door *clang-clanged* on the bars once more. "Hey." he said.

"What?" Eric said coldly.

"How you doing Quintus?" Morné said casually.

"Alright I guess. My sister is getting married."

"Tertia?"

"No Virginia."

"Oh, not for long, eh?" They shared a laugh which left Eric bewildered. Morné noticed his son's confusion: "Sorry, Quintus here was my escort to prison a while back."

"You got a good father there." the guard said to Eric. "You should have written him."

"Well I did actually. Several times but—this is not your business."

"I saved his life." Morné said to Eric, while smiling at the now-blushing guard. "Don't be shy; tell the story."

He looked back to the entrance, checking if the coast was clear. "Well we were riding to Rome. He was to be taken to Florence to serve his time for insurrection—"

"Would have been killed but I was a priest and it was a first offense so they let me live." Morné interjected.

"Anyway, we were crossing the Arno bridge and the wagon wheel broke. The horse was spooked and it fell into the water—"

"Freezing water, but beautiful. As blue as sapphire. Lovely town too."

"Well I can't swim—"

"Not a bit. Can't even float, this one. Just sank like a rock."

"It was all the armor you see—"

"Lucky too; I grabbed hold of some leather strap that was holding something metal to him and I paddled and paddled and worked us both to the shore."

"I passed out—" the guard said sheepishly.

"I thought he was dead but I wasn't sure, so I dragged him to the nearest Inn—"

This time it was Eric who interrupted: "And paid for a room plus extra, just like the Good Samaritan."

"I—no." Morné said, looking at him funny. "I didn't have any money Eric, I was a prisoner..." he looked round the room before adding: "I charged the room to the Pope!" he said with a great wheezing laugh.

"Anyway, they found us a day later and we took him on his way."

Morné chuckled again. "Everyone was so impressed that I hadn't tried to run for it, but I told them I was an old man and wasn't going to be getting far in Florence on foot. Lovely town though."

"Oh don't be modest. You could have

THE LADY IN THE LAKE

escaped if you wanted."

"Well maybe..."

The jailor sighed a great, pained exhale. Eric opened his mouth to speak but his father squeezed his fingers into his leg, silencing him. He wanted the quiet to linger, to let the jailor think.

"Tell you what..." the guard said, fumbling for his ring of keys. "I'll think of something, but...I just believe in paying back what's been given. So..." he turned the key and opened the door.

"They'll kill you for this, you know." Morné said.

"Yeah, well...I should've been dead already, right?"

"Maybe..." Morné said, placing his hand on the guard's shoulder. "Or maybe you lived back then, for just such a moment as this."

They stepped toward the door, with Eric focusing on where the rest of his group was being held. He didn't even notice the door in front of him creaking open as he slowly approached it. It wasn't till his dad grabbed his arm that he looked up to see the Inquisitor and two Templar standing in front of him.

"Or maybe you could give me a weapon?" Eric said, turning to the guard who'd just set him free. The Templar pulled a dagger from his belt and handed it over, while drawing his sword to face down his two comrades. The Inquisitor backed out and Morné backed out of the way, while the quartet of armed men converged and fought.

Eric had more experience—and from the look of his opponent, he also had a dozen years on him at least—and his smaller weapon was a better tool for the cramped setting; he disposed of his foe with haste. Quintus, however, was barely holding his own. Both he and his adversary were striking the stone walls more than anything else, but when Eric found an opening he seized it and plunged his dagger into the exposed neck of the Templar.

"Come on." Eric said after picking up the fallen Knight's sword. He whipped around to the door and burst into the next room.

"Eric!" Marcella shouted. She was occupying a cell on the right side of the room. Fortigo was on the left.

"Eric, they've got Dun and Jay and we think maybe Petro!" Fortigo said. The bars on his door were bent apart but the space was still to small for the giant to squeeze through. Quintus quickly unlocked his cell. Good thing too, as the entrance door opened a moment later and two more Templar rushed inside, swords drawn and ready. Fortigo reacted to them with a roar. He grabbed the bars of his cell and ripped the door free, chucking it at them as they charged for him. Pinned to the ground, Eric ran them both through with his sword.

"Why didn't you just rip the door off its

THE LADY IN THE LAKE

hinges earlier? Why try and squeeze the bars?" Marcella asked Fortigo as she jogged over to join them.

"Oh you know I never thought to until just then."

"Where are the others?" Eric asked.

"Outside. I saw they had something set up just outside the door. That's where they took Dun. I saw Jay out there last time they opened the door."

The group crept to the outside door and opened it just enough to see outside. "Oh." Eric said bluntly. The remaining Templar—six of them—plus the Inquisitor and Sal next to him, were standing, watching the door as if waiting for Eric to join them. He opened the door the rest of the way and stepped outside. Jay was strapped to the barrel he'd been hiding in earlier. Dun was nearby, still in his carrying bag, looking stone-faced, almost bored. Petro too was lingering nearby, his hands tied behind his back, but his expression blank. *Still putting on a front, even now*, Eric thought as he saw him.

"Don't turn around." Morné whispered to him from behind. "I wanted you to know it's okay."

"What's okay?" Eric asked, barely moving his lips.

"We're okay." he said, before brushing past Eric to approach the mob in front of them.

"You'll get your turn." the Inquisitor said. "He goes first."

"You gonna kill a boy?" Morné said, still slowly approaching the group.

"This is not a killing, it's a purging. Sin must be purged and it will be, from the least of them..." he dragged his hand from Jay's head to point to Eric. "...to the greatest of them."

Eric hurled an expletive at him that will not be repeated.

"And what about my boy?" Morné asked.

"Well despite what your other son said, he will not be killed. We value loyalty and faithfulness and he has shown that to the holy Father."

"It'll be alright dad, just sit tight." Sal said, nodding to his father who continued inching toward them, on small step at a time. His powder-blue robe was scuffed and dirty, ripped in places and off-kilter, with one baggy sleeve barely reaching his wrist while the other completely covered his hand. "It'll all be over soon." Sal said.

"Yes it will." the Inquisitor agreed. "Do you think—" Morné was close enough to reach out and touch him, but instead of doing that he lunged for him, right hand wrapped around a dagger he took from a dead Templar inside the jail. The blade sliced through the air, aimed right for the Inquisitor's heart, but it never reached its target.

THE LADY IN THE LAKE

Morné was too slow, the Templar next to his master was too fast and the old man's thin wrist was seized and the blade fell out of his hand only a second after it was exposed. The Inquisitor caught the falling blade in his hand and twirled it around so that its tip was pointed at the old man's chest.

Eric stepped forward but stopped as the Templar drew his sword and held it up, threateningly. There was no getting to him in time, Eric knew.

"You are no killer." the Inquisitor said.

"Dad back away!" Sal shouted, but his father did not move.

"And you are no priest." Morné said.

The Inquisitor only shrugged and plunged the knife in. Sal dove for him but only managed to catch him in his arms after he'd already been stabbed. They hit the ground together, with Sal too shaken to speak and Morné gently rubbing his coarse head of hair.

"Where is the Magistrate?" the Inquisitor asked the Templar to his left. "Hiding under his bed I suppose. Someone go and fish him out. Let him know one building will burn every hour until they surrender their allegiance to France and pledge themselves servants of the Holy Empire. I don't expect it will take many hours."

"Yes sir." one of the white Knights behind him said and jogged away, toward the row of houses perched up the road.

"What about this one?" another Templar said, stepping forward and pointing to Jay, still tied to the barrel.

"Right...well, on second thought put them in those iron carriages." The Inquisitor pointed to the grey prisoner's wagons that were parked outside the jailhouse. "Let's take them all back to Rome. Let the Emperor's justice be served in person."

Fortigo seemed ready to fight; Jay too looked eager the moment they cut him free. Marcella had to settle them both down immediately. This was not the time. Eric, meanwhile, was on the ground, staring at his father's limp body, still wrapped in the arms of Sal, whose weeping Eric could see but not hear; the sound was muffled by a ringing in his ears. A pair of hands hoisted him up and helped him inside the carriage, along with Petro and Jay. The door creaked and slammed shut, startling Eric, who finally snapped out of his haze.

"Now what?" Jay asked.

"We wait." Petro said, echoing Marcella's command to them.

"No." Eric said, his voice surprisingly level and sober. "We're going to kill every last one of them. Immediately."

THE LADY IN THE LAKE

MATTHEW L. MARTIN
CHAPTER 10 : MOTHER AND SON

The battle ended with a well-organized retreat. Say what you want about Sir Richard—this **was** his first time commanding troops on a battlefield in a good decade—the man can organize a solid retreat. He had English troops in formation, tucking tails and marching away with all the rigidity and etiquette of finely tuned military machine. The Scots and Irish didn't even give chase, instead they watched their conquered enemies abandon the battlefield, yield England's northern country from York to Scot's Land, and return home with wounded prides.

King Fenial allowed his counterpart Mordred to return to Camelot as well. A different

THE LADY IN THE LAKE

King might've kept such a rich prize as a captive, but Fenial knew he'd won, and not just the battle; he could see it all over Mordred's face before the fighting even began. "He's a broken boy." Fenial said to his counselors, a few of which dared to protest allowing Mordred to go free. "Not long for his throne. If I wanted I could march an army to Dover and conquer everything along the way; he'd barely stir. Let him be. The weight of his crown will kill him even easier than I could."

*****

A few hours after the battle was ended, Mordred opened his eyes in his royal carriage. He was alone; no advisor or counselor was with him, offering him advice or counsel. No one was there to tell him what went wrong, what to do next or when to carry out their next plan...whatever that would be. He sat up and rubbed the sleep out of his eyes, peering out the window to see fields of green rolling by. He had no idea where he was; the English countryside always looked the same to him from Manchester to London.

It took him a moment to remember the end of the battle, but a sudden shooting pain in his side. His hand jerked toward it instinctively, sliding under this tattered tabard to run his fingers over the rigid pattern of hastily sewn skin. *Hanbury*, he remembered, *...and Oxlef, of course*. It came back to him all at once, betrayal on top of betrayal. He recalled the sight of the battle lost—over half the English slaughtered—and his declaration of surrender. What followed he did not know, *but I'm alive and clearly unshackled so my freedom is at least secured. Back to Camelot I suppose...*

The rain had relented though a sticky humidity made the ride that much more uncomfortable. Days they travelled from York to Camelot, with Mordred too weary to leave his carriage other than to relieve himself. He had little interaction with anyone. A quarterman would bring him meals and on one occasion a Knight approached to tell him how many days they had left to travel. He spotted Sir Richard near a campfire one evening and he called to his counselor-Knight from his carriage, but the Knight seemed not to hear him and moments later stepped away toward a tent.

Finally their procession reached a path Mordred recognized; *almost home,* he told himself. The wagon bumped along the uneven terrain that snaked toward his Camelot castle, to his mother, to his RoundTable, to his throne, to Rose...to someone—anyone—who could give him answers, a strategy, something to turn the tables and win...*If I am to go out, I want it to be with a victory*, he thought to himself, though he did not dwell on what it meant to "go out." That was a decision he was not risking even to think about until the time was right.

THE LADY IN THE LAKE

"Your grace." a Knight said, opening his carriage door. "some of your RoundTable are conversing, if you would like to join them…" He held a hand out in the direction of a trio of figures, half-obscured under the fading sunset. Their procession had stopped near a forested brook that Mordred knew was only an hour from Camelot.

"Why are we here?" he asked the Knight, though the soldier did not have an answer, only an awkward look over to the trio of counselors huddled nearby. Mordred shuffled slowly toward them, still weary from his stabbing and loss of blood. "My Lords and Knights, why—"

"Shh!" Sir White snapped at him.

"Your grace it is not safe to speak so loudly." Sir Maris said.

"We are at the edge of Camelot's estate, what is the danger?!" Mordred whispered.

"Return to your carriage; we will handle this." Sir Grummore said.

"Handle what?!"

Instead of answering, Sir White motioned for a Knight to join them. The soldier jogged over at once, nodding to his superior but giving no acknowledgement to his King. "Take his majesty back to his carriage. Secure it…for his protection." White said.

"Wait, I—" Mordred began but stopped to wince at his injured side; the guard had his large hand wrapped around the King's arm and was almost dragging him back to his carriage. "Wait a moment, Knight, I am your King!" Mordred shouted, prompting another flurry of "shush's" from the trio of Lords.

"Are you?" the Knight said, helping Mordred—not gently—back inside. He slammed the door shut and motioned for two more soldiers to assist them. "This door does not open." he said to his companions, who nodded and pressed their backs against the door, to ensure Mordred did not slip away.

"Shh!" rang another shout before Mordred could even protest further.

"I didn't say anything!" he said, more than annoyed at being treated like a servant.

"Halt!" another soldier shouted and Mordred instantly realized there was more going on than he knew.

"Drop your weapons and surrender." a new voice responded, calm and commanding.

"Stand aside or there will be bloodshed." the soldier demanded. Apparently the man did not heed his command because the unmistakable sound of charging feet and shouted war-cries reverberated around the scene. The clang of steel against steel rang out as well as shouts from various people all around, but after only seconds of mayhem the wooded area fell silent.

"He's in there." the voice of Sir White said. Mordred did not know who exactly the "he" was

THE LADY IN THE LAKE

in that sentence but he had a pretty good guess and sure enough, seconds later the soldiers who had been standing guard beside his carriage stepped aside and the door swung open to reveal:

"Terance." Mordred said. "Traitor." he spat; literally spitting at the tall Knight's mustachioed face.

"I didn't put my blade in your side." he said with a sneer.

"You and Hanbury do everything together. He is guilty and so you are as well."

"Well…maybe." Terance said, stepping back to allow a pair of Knights to lean into the carriage and drag Mordred out. "It doesn't really matter now, does it?"

"Where is Sir Richard?" Mordred demanded, but no one cared enough to answer. A pommel jabbed him in the back and the stumbled forward right as the caravan slowly began moving. He looked back to assess the situation but ate another jab to the back.

"Walk." the guard said.

"I have a carriage if you want me to go to my Castle." The Knight did not respond. The colors and emblem on his tabard was barely visible in the early evening light, but a red harp was a red harp; Mordred knew the sigil well. "You serve the House of Ander? Then Baudwin is your Lord, yes? Baudwin is a loyal subject. You disgrace…why are you laughing?!"

It wasn't just the one; the whole lot of them were barking a loud and mocking laughter at the King. He wanted to protest further, to turn around and demand answers, but every time he tried, he suffered a stab in the back with the pommel of the guard's sword. After a few minutes he gave up. After an hour they reached the gates of Camelot, which were guarded by more Knights of cherry red and white, adorned with harps on their chests.

Mordred was led into the Great Hall of his own Castle, where he found another man sitting in his throne. "Lord Baudwin?" he asked, dumbfounded by the sight. The old Lord looked every bit a man of seventy. His great walrus-like mustache was solid white, and the last bits of hair he had left looked like ivory strings pouring out of the back of his head. He was still fat though; age could not diminish that round belly.

"Mordred, son of Arthur. You are relieved from your responsibility as sovereign over the English Empire." It was a moment before the young man processed what he'd just been told, and even once he did, he still failed to understand what exactly was happening. It's not everyday a coup d'état happens, after all.

The entrance of his RoundTable distracted him entirely from the matter at hand, however. Nine men entered behind Baudwin, forming a half-moon formation to his right. Mordred looked them over, one after the other. Dondal was

THE LADY IN THE LAKE

absent—*killed by the Scots, no doubt*—and Hanbury was as well—*killed by me*—but the rest were accounted for. Even Sir Terance had the temerity to show his face, as did—

"Oxlef!" Mordred lunged toward the Lord Knight but the soldier behind him quickly seized him, dragging him back to his place in front of Baudwin's throne. "That man betrayed us!" Mordred cried. "He turned his forces against England and sided with Fenial!"

"Turned against you, not England." Oxlef said. "I make a motion for this RoundTable to legitimize Lord Baudwin and recognize his right to claim the throne by conquest."

"I concur." Sir Terance quickly added.

"On what grounds?" Sir Richard piped in. He was standing at the end of the row of men, a step or two away from the group as though he did not entirely belong. "What royal claim does he hold? What conquest did he do?"

"Is there no objection?" Sir Oxlef said, acting as if Richard had not spoken at all. "None?"

"Very well, shall we vote?" Terance said, raising his right hand in support of Baudwin. Oxlef followed immediately after, while the others looked left and right amongst themselves, wordlessly debating.

"This is no takeover!" Richard shouted, though his yells continued to be ignored. "This is petty politics!" He loosened the leather strap holding his scabbard in place and drew his sword, dropping its holster to the ground. The RoundTable did not stir, but a dozen guards around the room drew their swords in response, freezing the Knight in place.

Sir White raised his hand in support, followed by Sir Grummore. They both looked to Sir Maris who turned away to meet the eyes of Mordred. "Sir Maris, you know what this is. You know what happened at York. There must be a way to—"

Maris raised his hand.

Sirs George, Loxley and Clarence followed after, succumb to the peer pressure around them. Only Richard remained the lone holdout.

"Very good. It's unanimous. Long life King Baudwin!"

Baudwin rose from his throne to nod in respect to his RoundTable. "Summon my son." he said, prompting an aid to hurry out of the Great Hall.

"Where's my mother?" Mordred asked, suddenly realizing she would not be the type to let something like this go without a response.

Baudwin did not answer him but instead pointed in his direction while looking at one of his guards: "And get this pathetic boy out of my Throne Room."

THE LADY IN THE LAKE

*****

Gwen was in the dungeon cell waiting for him. The black streak under her eye indicated she'd put up a fight and suffered a vicious backhand for her trouble. "Mother." he said as they threw up into the cell opposite hers.

"Are you hurt?" she asked him before he could ask her.

"A little." He pulled up his shirt to reveal the poor stitching job that had been done to him soon after the battle. "Do you know what happened?" he asked, thinking about the coup and not the battle. Gwen took him to mean the battle, however.

"I know you lost. Something about the Welsh turning against you."

"Against us." he insisted. "Against England."

"It doesn't matter. Baudwin had the Castle taken before we even received word of your defeat."

"How?"

"He marched in with his army, said he had business with me."

"And you let him in the gates?!"

"How was I supposed to know he meant to conquer?!"

"He came with his army!" Mordred was on his feet, gripping he bars of his cell, completely forgetting that he made more than his fair share of blunders recently. Now he had reason to blame someone else for his problems and he was seizing the opportunity.

"He's only ever been loyal. He helped me once before, I had no reason not to trust him."

"Wrong." a third voice echoed from the doorway that exited the dungeons. A tall and armored figure stood facing them, hair a mess of black with a pointed goatee to match. He stepped toward them, letting his visage glow in the dim torchlights hanging from the wall. He wore a plain white tabard, unscathed by any battle, and gripped a silver sword that hung from his belt. "Had you considered for even a moment the circumstances of my father's help twenty years ago, you'd never have opened a gate. You'd have opened fire on him."

"Who are you?" Mordred asked.

"Lot?" Gwen said. She always knew the families of the various Lords better than her son.

"You took advantage of my father's generosity—"

"As I recall his help came very begrudgingly. I wouldn't call it generosity."

"He didn't want to help associates with pagans."

"Pagans?!"

"That wizard who counseled your husband. It's his fault the witch returned with Kason. And its your fault for letting him stay and hold the ear the King Arthur."

"Do not speak my husband's name."

"Your **first** husband's." Lot said coldly. "Does this one know? Does he know what is whispered behind his royal back?"

"Know what? What is whispered? What does that mean?" Mordred asked.

"There's nothing **to** know. Whispers are for cowards."

"So are lies, Queen mother." He let his words hang for a moment before resuming. "My father has the throne but he is not long for life. He secured it for me, his last act to try and create for me a better world than what you and your wizard friends gave him."

"I don't have wizard friends. I haven't even seen Merlin in years!"

Lot's dismissive wave indicated he wasn't interested in debating, only in lecturing. "They say the Old Lands are bubbling like a cauldron of pepper stew, about to blow. There's talk of witches and warlocks and other of their kind picking sides for a great battle. I imagine you'd have your son lead England into such a mess."

"I don't even know what—"

"It's not going to happen now." He turned to exit but stopped to offer one last word. "The Sons of Britain were right you know? My father and I have had a long time to think about it. All they wanted was to give power to the proudest, fiercest and best people on the Island. Look at your son? Does he qualify?"

"He is the King." she said, defending her son who remained silent and confused.

"Was." Lot said as he slammed the iron door behind him. His shadow disappeared behind the small window, as another figure replaced him, the guard assigned to keep watch over the prisoners.

*****

Mordred woke up hours later, though how much time exactly had passed he did not know (they don't keep clocks in the dungeons). It had hardly been a peaceful night's sleep as he kept walking up at the sound of a mouse scratching around his cell. After an hour of it, he finally rolled over to shoo the creature away, only to discover the sound was coming from his mother as she worked to cut her dress on a jagged rock sticking out of the wall of her cell.

"What are you doing?" he asked her.

"What does it look like? I'm escaping."

"How?"

With a sigh of relief she managed to rip a tear in the bottom of her dress, allowing her to work the tear around her body, turning her long, formal gown into something much shorter and thus more revealing. "Like that." she said before turning to the door. "Hey!" The shadow behind

THE LADY IN THE LAKE

the door turned slightly but did not open. "Guard! Hey!" The iron door creaked open and a shadow stood facing them. "There we go." Gwen said, standing just such a way as to be as enticing as one could be. The figure stepped forward, revealing herself to be a guard not like Gwen was expecting. "Oh...well that's very progressive."

"Quiet." she said.

"Wait!" Gwen said. "Do you, uh...I mean, how progressive are you?" The guard turned back to her, smirking slightly. "There you go." A moment later she was fumbling with the keys to unlock Gwen's cell door.

Two moments later Gwen was pouncing. Leaping onto the guard as she entered the cell, Gwen's knees drove into her chest and forced her to the ground. Instantly her legs were around the guard's neck, cutting off her air supply as she struggled and flailed. Soon after the guard was out, flopping her arms down as her body fell limp and unconscious.

Mordred was shocked. Gwen approached his cell door with keys in hand and noticed his incredulous expression. "For the record, I was going to do that regardless if they were a man or a woman."

"I didn't know you knew how to do that? When did you learn how to do that?"

"This is not my first time in a jail cell, son. Let's go."

There was no guard keeping watch outside of the dungeon. Gwen opened the door slowly to have a look down the long hallway. Camelot's dungeon was an oversized subterranean ant-colony, with a dozen hallways branching away from the main-path, each ending in a square room that held two cells each. The intent was to create a place where prisoners could be held while also limiting their interaction with each other. Assuming the dungeon was fully manned by the correct number of guards, each hallway would have lookouts stationed at each entrance to the main hallway.

"There's no way to know if his place is crawling with guards or if she was the only one." Gwen said, peering down the hall at each of the iron doors that led to their own respective hallways.

"Why wouldn't there be?" Mordred asked, though immediately he felt as if he should have already known the answer, being a King and all. Fortunately Gwen exercised the kind of patience only a mother would offer her son.

"Because there's been a change in power. That usually means little things like staff assignments get lost in the shuffle. Let's hope so, at least."

They slipped out of their cell room and into the exposed hallway. It was a straight shot to the stairway, past six doors on either side of them, each with a window cut into them. They crouched under the windows on the right of the isle, fully exposed to any guard who might peer out of the windows on their left. None did however, and they reached the stairs soon after without any alarm.

The jingle of keys hitting a stone floor stopped them in their tracks not three steps into their ascent. Instinctively they whipped around to see a brown face peering through one of the windows halfway down the hall.

"Sir Richard!" Mordred shouted, rushing to him as he unlocked the door. "We didn't know they had you."

"They had me until the morning. Then I was to be killed."

"Madness." Gwen said. "Come with us, we need all the help we can get."

"Where are we going?" Mordred asked.

"To the other dungeon." Gwen said, slack-faced. There was a look of pitiful resignation in her eyes as she knew what she had to do but was not fully prepared to do it. "Like I said, we need all the help we can get." she added, more to herself than her companions.

"What makes you so sure his grace's brother will assist us. He's been locked away for a very long time." Richard said, and it was only then that Mordred realized what his mother's plan was.

"No mother. Leave him be."

"I can't do that. They will kill him…or worse."

"Let him die then!" the boy-King snapped.

"I won't take a side, your highness," Richard said, "but I will say again that we don't know how he'll behave if we set him loose."

"My son will follow my instruction; I'm not worried about that." Gwen said. *"But I won't lie…It's what he may do after we let him free that concerns me." There was no time for debate, however. Worried though she was, it was her only play.* We have only a day, if not less, Gwen thought to herself.

Within a day, Baudwin will complete his takeover of the surrounding area. Within a week word will spread that he and Lot have taken the throne. By that time propaganda will spread and Lordships will fall in line. When that happens the new normal will take hold.

"Mother?" Mordred asked, squeezing her arm and pulling her back to reality.

Gwen was lingering at the top of the stairs, her hand resting on the iron door. Directly across from the courtyard beyond was the stable house and the only access to her second son's crypt, where he's been chained and restrained for the better part of twenty years.

"We have to act now." she said, setting her eyes on the stable and letting her inner monologue slip out of her lips. "And Kilgara is our only hope."

THE LADY IN THE LAKE

MATTHEW L. MARTIN
CHAPTER 11 : GENIE IN A BOTTLE

Merlin's eyes opened to see the beady, watery eyes of Rumpel so close to his face their eyebrows were almost interlocked. "Gah!" the wizard shouted, scooting backwards to put some separation between he and the loathsome conman. "How long have I been out?" he asked, rubbing his short hair and matching whiskers.

"Three years." Rumpel replied with a grave and somber tone.

"What?!"

"No, I'm kidding. We just got here. You hit your head pretty hard when we popped in; must've knocked you loopy for a minute."

"What about you?"

THE LADY IN THE LAKE

"Oh I landed on you, I'm fine."

"Where are we?" Merlin asked as he pulled himself up to look around. It looked like a cave dug into the side of a mountain. The floor and walls were uneven and stalactites loomed ominously overhead. The only thing unnatural to be seen was a large door fixed to the wall opposite them, though there was no handle or lever to be found, only a plain square window, slightly above Merlin's eye level. "Last thing I remember were three foul looking men coming…coming for **you** as I recall." He glowered at the little man with contemptuous eyes.

"Now wait a minute. I'll thank you to resist the urge to blame me for this."

"This is your fault!"

"No, no, if anything it's both of our faults. If you want to get technical the fact we're **here** is yours, the fact they came looking for me is mine."

"How is it my fault we're here?! I don't even know where we are!"

"I'm going to guess we're in the dungeon of MadSu. You know, the guardian of this land!"

"I'm still waiting for which part of this is my fault." Merlin said, hands on his hips like a parent scolding a child.

"I told you not to use magic after they threw down that…thing they have. Once it starts spinning you have to get away from it or it'll suck you up and spit you out here."

"You said no such thing."

"Did too!"

"Did not, I have a perfect memory of the event. It was on page 122 that you said 'whatever you do, don't—' but you never said anything after the dash. We were interrupted and ended up here.

"Interrupted by YOU! You whipped out your wand and cast a spell before I could stop you."

"So fine then." Merlin said confidently. "It's both our faults."

A female voice interrupted their argument. "A little right and a little wrong." she said. Merlin and Rumpel spun around to face the door, discerning a shadow behind the window. The door creaked open and in stepped a woman with amber skin, dark brown hair and a look of supreme contempt.

"I demand to be released!" Rumpel said, pointing a stubby finger at Merlin. "He's the one you want. Magic user, that one is. I'm just a commoner."

"You are in no position to demand anything of me." she said, stepping toward him with a frame that doubled his own. "Nor are you just a commoner."

Merlin cleared his throat and removed his hat. "MadSu, I am—"

"Save it; I'll deal with you next." she snapped, still focused on Rumpel.

THE LADY IN THE LAKE

"I'm telling you…you've got the wrong man." Rumpel's eyes welled-up and his lip quivered. It was almost believable.

"Do I? Tell me troll, do you know where you are right now?"

"Y—your dungeon?"

"I don't have a dungeon, try again."

"I was told you kidnap wizards and throw them in your dungeon…"

"No. I don't bother keeping what is not fit to live. Now…try again."

"I—I don't know."

"Amazing." she said, shaking her head. "So you did all this…" she stretched her hands around the empty room. But for a stack of straw in the corner there was nothing to see. "and you don't even recognize it as your handiwork. I find that…highly unlikely."

A lightbulb flashed in Rumpel's brain. His mouth slipped open and his finger pointed to the mound of straw in the corner behind him. "You mean this…that was **your** gold?"

"That was **my** gold!" she confirmed with a deranged shout, picking him up by his jacket cuff and hurling him into the stack of straw. "Who did you **think** you were stealing from?!"

"Not you, obviously! Do I look like an idiot! I thought…wait," Rumpel looked again around the barren room, "is this the castle?!"

"This is the vault. The vault!" She shoved

him aside and grabbed a handful of the straw. "And this is all that's left of my gold!"

"I swear, I thought this castle was abandoned. I checked everywhere for an occupant!"

Merlin couldn't help himself but scoff. "You found a castle full of gold and you just assumed someone forgot about it?"

"You stay out of this." Rumpel said.

"You will bring my gold back. All of it."

"I—I—I can't, my magic doesn't work that way!"

"Well then you'd better learn because when I return it had better be to a vault full of gold bars."

She turned to exit but Rumpel shouted once more time: "What do you want with gold, anyway?!" She did not respond but instead stepped out of the door, closing it behind her with a creak and a *click.*

She turned back to utter one last threat through the window in the door: "As for you, wizard, when I come back it will be for **your** head as well."

A brief moment of silence fell between the two men. Merlin looked happy to let the silence linger but Rumpel was too panic-stricken and desperate to escape to stop and calmly formulate a plan.

Like a rat he scurried over to the corners of

THE LADY IN THE LAKE

the room, scratching and clawing at the stones, hoping to find some weak spot he might exploit, anything to break through and wiggle away. When that failed he turned his attention to the small window in the door, trying desperately to squeeze his small frame through. It was no use, however.

"Let me get this straight." Merlin said with a sigh. "You've been gallivanting all over MadSu's land, swindling poor farmers out of booze, telling them you can turn straw into gold."

"Basically." Rumpel said, leaping down from the window with a pant. "What's your point?"

"But you can't do anything of the sort; you've just been swapping out the farmers' hay and straw for the guardian's gold."

"Your point?"

"So you have **some** magical ability but clearly you're just a charlatan."

"That's the short of it yes. What's your **point**?"

Merlin smirked a self-satisfied grin. "I just think it's funny: My specialty is transformation. I actually **can** turn that straw into gold."

"You can!" Rumpel's eyes widened as he inched closer to the tall magician. "Do it already!"

"I can also blink out of here as effortlessly as she did just now."

"Yes! Let's go then!"

"No. I can't."

"Wha—you just said."

"I can **ordinarily** but there's something preventing me from using my magic. It's quite unusual. I've been in similar situations before but not quite like this." Rumpel had no response except to kick the pile of straw in juvenile frustration. A tuff of the stuff fluttered into the air and lazily descended, which only seemed to enrage the little man more. He kicked again, trying to release some aggression. "We're not going to get out of here with you kicking straw or pounding sand or whatever other metaphor you want to use. We need a—"

clang

"What was that?" Rumpel said, freezing in place with his right foot stuck out in front of him.

"You kicked something." Merlin knelt down and began rummaging through the pile of straw, emerging a moment later with a small oil lamp in his hands. "Eureka." he mumbled to himself.

"What's that? What'd you say?"

"Jenny." he replied.

"That's not what you said." But he lost interest in arguing as he became instantly transfixed on the lamp. It looked like a squashed, silver kettle.

"Do you know what this is?" Merlin asked.

"Yes." Rumpel lied.

"Then use it." Merlin said, holding it out for

THE LADY IN THE LAKE

him to take.

"Don't be stupid I don't have any tea bags."

"I thought not. Let's try rubbing it." And without stopping to explain he rubbed the side of the lamp with his large sleeve, as if trying to scrub away a smudge. The silver began to glow red, like a great fire was suddenly raging inside. Red steam poured out of the spout and wisped into the air, twisting and curling and forming the shape of a torso, arms and head.

"Jenny." Merlin said, looking up at the great red figure. Rumpel was backed against the opposite wall, either terrified or bewildered, it was all the same.

"Can you not?" the large red man replied. "I prefer to be called Genie, like the peanut butter."

"Can you get us out of here?" Rumpel asked from the other side of the room.

"Maybe. Which one of you set me free?"

"I did." Merlin said

"I found you, though! Set us both free!"

"Alright. I will grant you both two wishes for releasing me from my containment."

"Two?" Rumpel said with obvious disappointment.

"One each. That seems fair."

"That's fine, we only need one wish anyway."

"Very good, one wish for the two of you. It is done."

"No no no!" Rumpel shouted, waving his hands and rushing toward the genie. "We will each take our own wish, thank you very much."

"Yes well, that **was** your first wish. He wished for one wish and got his one wish."

"Oh my, that really is very well reasoned." Merlin said, nodding his head, impressed.

"Now it is your turn to wish." the genie said to Rumpel.

"Alright, let me see."

"Wait. First let me tell you the rules."

"What rules? Merlin didn't get any rules."

"Merlin is more trustworthy than you are. First, I can not raise the dead."

"Fine fine, no problem." Rumpel said, waving his hand to hurry the genie along.

"Second, I can not take you backwards or forwards in time."

"Okay that's fine."

"Third, I can not grant extra wishes. I'm not an idiot."

"Heh." Rumpel muttered under his breath. He'd been thinking about that one.

"Very well then? Good. What is your wish."

"Well let's not overcomplicate things. Get me out! Leave Merlin but get me out!"

"Hey!" Merlin said, offended by the sudden betrayal.

The room shook slightly but nothing else happened. Rumpel and Merlin held their arms out

THE LADY IN THE LAKE

to steady their balance. After a moment, the quake ended with everyone still very much in the locked room. "Alas I can not." the genie said simply.

"Fine then take Merlin too."

"No, there is a magic here that prevents me…worry not, though; that won't count as your wish."

"Better get creative." Merlin said.

"Fine, just give me a moment to think."

"Is that your wish—?"

"No! I'll tell you when I'm ready." Rumpel snapped. The genie nodded as the little gnome paced the room. Time was running out, they knew. MadSu could return at any moment. He had to be smart, clever, deceptive even… "I've got it!"

"You are ready for your wish?"

"Yes…make another one of us."

"Another…"

"No." Merlin said. "I want no part of this."

"Fine. Make another one of **me** then. See, when MadSu comes back…" Rumpel moved around the room, acting the scenario out for his benefit more than the genie's. "She'll see…me…the other me that is. And when she steps forward to kill him, I'll slip out the door and escape. It's brilliant!"

"Your wish is for another one of you?"

"That's right."

"I've never granted such a wish before. Give me a…" the genie paused for a moment as he trailed off, looking over his shoulder as though he felt someone lingering there. Merlin looked too but saw nothing.

"What is it?" Merlin asked. "What do you feel?"

"It's nothing I just thought…It's nothing. Now then, another one of you."

"Yes, hurry!" Rumpel said, looking over his own shoulder, certain that MadSu would be bursting in any moment.

"Give me a moment to consider how…"

"There's no time!"

Merlin was getting a bad feeling. It had hit him around the same time the genie felt something in the room. Magi have that sort of sixth sense, when they can feel the presence of something or someone unsavory lingering nearby. It's not an exact science and sometimes it doesn't work at all, but when it does it gives them all the willies. "Rumpel I don't think—" he began, but was once more cut off by the impatient gnome.

"Just do it!" he shouted and, as if answering his request, the genie vanished in a puff of smoke, colored yellow and mingled with red.

"This is a bad idea—" Merlin began again but was once more interrupted as the genie reappeared. His eyes were glossed over and his expression was blank but Rumpel didn't care. Merlin inhaled as if to speak, but Rumpel shushed him before he could. The genie scrunched his face

THE LADY IN THE LAKE

and crossed his arms, contemplating how to perform the task. Finally he nodded. With a snap of his fingers a blinding light flashed in the room. When Merlin and Rumpel's eyes adjusted, they realized the genie was gone. For several seconds everything remained quiet.

Another flash of blinding light appeared around them and the genie returned, with a small gnomish looking man at his side. Rumpel looked his clone over with a scrutinizing eye. The doppelganger meanwhile looked utterly confused. He seemed to recognize Rumpel, however, though he was either unwilling or unable to speak.

"He doesn't look exactly like me…" Rumpel said, squinting an eye as he looked the double over. "His nose is a little taller and his beard's a little thinner….it'll do." he finally said "Alright, back in the can." The genie did not hesitate; his half-vaporous self twisted and twirled and sucked itself back into the lamp.

Right around that time the click-clack of approaching footfall alerted them. Rumpel raced to the spot where the door would open. Merlin joined him. The door creaked and opened, revealing MadSu, who stepping into the room with a long staff in her hands. "You have failed," she said, "like I knew you would. Where is the wizard?" She looked around the room but by the time she did, they had already slipped away, out of the room, down the hall, through the ruined old castle, and away from the magic-suppressing charm she'd placed over the perimeter.

"Take me to my house!" Rumpel shouted. Without hesitation Merlin grabbed his arm and whisked him away. They reappeared a moment later on the edge of a windy, forest-covered path with small cottages peppered all around.

"This it?" Merlin said, looking around.

"Close enough. Well, bye!" Rumpel said, starting quickly down the road. Merlin's long arm seized him once again how.

"I'm coming with you."

"Why?"

"Because once we check on your family you're coming back with me. We're going to make things right with MadSu."

"Make—you can't make things right with her! She's insane, surely you saw that yourself. She's been hunting your kind for ages!"

"Our kind." Merlin corrected him as they started down the path. "She seems quite free of prejudice on that account. Nevertheless I think she can be persuaded to join my cause, assuming I can state my case to her. In the meantime, lets go and tell your wife and children you are okay. I'm sure they've been worried after you've been gone so long."

A few minutes of walking (a mild bickering) ended with Rumpel picking up the pace as he neared a particular cottage perched on a hill to

THE LADY IN THE LAKE

their right.

"Wife!" he called as he burst through the door. There was no answer. He pulled out the genie lamp and placed it on the dining table. Inspecting the house, he found his wife in his son's room, crying alone on his child-sized bed. "What is it? What's happened!" Merlin slowly entered behind them, head bowed.

"Our son!" she said, through her wailing.

"What of him?!"

"He is taken!

Rumpel stood quietly for pregnant moment, shocked. Finally he asked: "How?!"

It took a moment for his wife to compose herself before speaking. "Some creature. Red and terrible." His heart sank at the description. "I was reading our son a bedtime story when he just appeared. He grabbed our son; put some kind of a spell on him."

"What kind of spell?"

"He turned him into a full-grown man." She grabbed his arm, wiping tears away. "He looked so handsome...like his father. And then...they were gone."

Rumpel ran to the dining table and rubbed the lamp.

"My master?" The genie said, half-appearing out of the issuing steam.

"My son! That was my son!"

"It was the best I could do; you were

pressed for time—"

"You should have told me! I would never—I want him back!"

"I'm sorry."

"No. You tricked me! Bring him back!"

"I cannot bring back the dead."

"...Then take me back!" Rumpel pleaded. "Let me do it ov—" The genie was already shaking his head 'no.'

"What kind of monster toys with people in such a way?" he asked meekly and defeated.

"You do, troll." the genie's voice responded, though the tone changed with every syllable. Rumpel looked up to see the genie's face changing to that of MadSu's. The woman stepped out of the steam, fully-formed, holding a long staff in one hand and the genie's lamp in the other. A puff of red smoke began to twist out of the spout but she stuck her thumb over it, denying the true genie the chance to emerge.

An unnatural glow was emanating from the end of her staff, flooding the room with a dull yellow light. "Consider your lesson learned." she said with an eerie calm.

"Is this how you function as a guardian?!" Merlin asked, shocked and appalled.

"I'm not here to be a guardian I am here to judge."

"Playing games with people, murdering innocent children? That's being a judge?"

THE LADY IN THE LAKE

"I didn't kill the child, magi. The troll did when he offered to sacrifice his life for the copy's."

"Are you mad? You swung the blade. You murdered an innocent—"

Indeed madness **was** in her eyes. "A life for a life. It was fair and impartial as the guardians are supposed to be, but also vengeful and fierce, as few guardians ever were."

"You are not even of my kind, are you?" Merlin asked her, stealthily letting his wand slide down his forearm (where he keeps it hidden in his sleeve) into his hand.

"No, but I have mastered the talents of your kind; exceeded them, even. And once I've ridden the world of the guardians and all other magic-wielders, the rest of us will finally rule as we were meant to."

"And when that day comes, I suppose you'll break that staff that gives you so much power, yes?" Merlin asked, but MadSu did not answer. Of course she would not lay down her power. "And here I thought you were simply a guardian with a big ego and a warped sense of self-righteousness. How disappointing."

"You're all disappointing to me." she snarled with contempt. "I know who you are; you're the lost guardian of France, been searching the world for people to join your quest to kill your sister."

"That's a bit over-simplified, but—"

"I'll kill her. And you. And every other—"

Merlin was quicker than she was. His wand was out, pointed and a spell fired before she even realized what was happening. With a *bang* the air molecules around MadSu were transformed into stones, solidifying and dropping around her, entombing her inside.

"Let's go." Rumpel said. He was stepping back into the dining room from his child's bedroom, eyes red and face blotchy. The swindler-conman had been crying genuine tears. Merlin never even noticed that he'd slipped off while he was conjuring the stone hedge around MadSu.

"Go? You should stay. I need to go. This thing won't hold her forever."

"Exactly." Rumpel said, slinging a bag over his back. "And when she gets out she's going to be coming for the both of us. I've said my goodbyes. I need to go to protect my family."

"Alright, but I warn you, the place we're going might also be dangerous. We can not just appear there, either. It must be sailed to."

"What place is it?"

"The home of my sister...my *other* sister. The good one, though we've not spoken in a while, I can't promise what kind of state she'll be in. Still, she's our only hope. She's the oldest and strongest of us. She can help."

"Fine. I'm ready." Rumpel said flatly as he strolled to his door. The stone box between them

THE LADY IN THE LAKE

began to rumble. "Hurry."

"We can cover **some** ground by magic." Merlin said. "A little distance won't hurt; I doubt even MadSu would challenge us where we're going."

He grabbed Rumpel's arm and in the blink of an eye they were both gone. Three seconds later the first stone fell from MadSu's upright coffin, and the tip of her staff broke through, freeing the guardian hunter once more as she resolved to track down the magis that had slipped past her, *for the last time*.

MATTHEW L. MARTIN
CHAPTER 12 : ABSOLUTION AND RESOLUTION

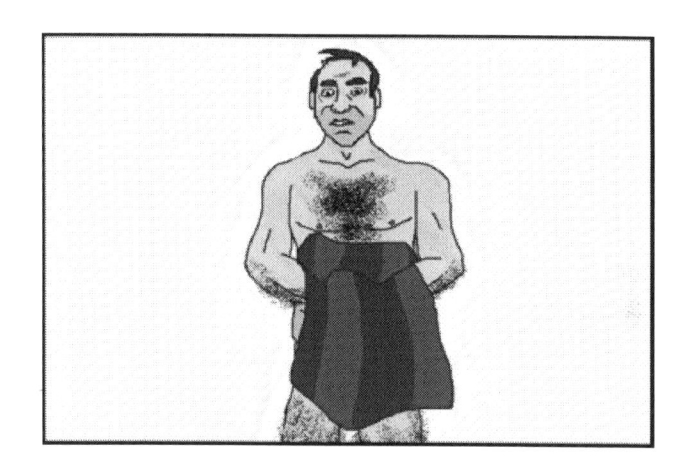

An hour passed before Eric spoke. The cramped prison wagon was even more cramped with Petro and Jay stretched out across from him. "I have an idea." Petro said, though Eric ignored him.

"Your ideas never work." Jay said, shifting as he sat. "Half my body is asleep right now." he complained.

"Better than Fortigo." Petro said, looking out the small, barred window at the end of the carriage.

"What do you mean?"

"They drug him out of his wagon and beat him up pretty bad about ten minutes ago."

"What's their strategy here?" Jay said, more annoyed than curious. "If they want to kill us just

THE LADY IN THE LAKE

do it. If not take us to Rome already.

"I doubt we're all going to Rome." Petro said gravely.

"Oh."

"They just want me." Eric finally said. "Maybe Marcella too…"

"Well it doesn't matter," Petro said as he patted Jay's arm. "Like I said, I have a plan."

"The last time you had a plan was were busted outside that club in Monaco—"

"That would have worked if you hadn't taken your wig off!"

"That crossing guard was making faces at me." Jay retorted, pale face blushing to match his red hair. "Not good faces."

"Booty call." Eric suddenly said. They both looked at him warily. "Booty call." he repeated, looking directly at Jay.

"No."

"Yes, it's perfect. There's three of us, small space."

"Last time we tried booty call, Fortigo almost crushed my ribcage."

"I'll be the perp this time." Eric said, raising his eyebrows as though he knew he just won the argument.

"I don't know…"

"You have a better plan to get out of here?"

"Booty call only works with Marcella."

"It's fine, Petro can be Marcella."

"Why am **I** Marcella?" Petro said, suddenly invested in the debate. "You should be Marcella. I'll be Eric."

"I'm already Eric. You be Marcella."

"This is crazy, I already **have** a plan." Petro tried to hold his arms out but Jay's body was in the way. "If you two would just give me room to stretch, you'll see—"

"We don't have time for your weird yoga poses or whatever you read in that book. This is the plan. Booty call." Eric's tone was final; the other two dropped the argument and nodded.

"Who's the mark?" Jay asked.

Petro peered out the window again. "There's an older one out there but he's harassing the other carriage right now. Best bet's the young one who's patrolling the space between us and Marcella's carriage."

"Alright," Eric said, pointing a finger at Jay. "this only works if it's convincing."

"I can take it. I'm read—"

WHAM

Eric drove his fist right into Jay's nose. Blood immediately began pouring down his face. "AH, that REALLY hurt! Why couldn't I just bite my tongue or something."

"This makes more blood. Say the line." Eric said.

"Right...I DON'T WANNA DIE! I DON'T

THE LADY IN THE LAKE

WANNA DIE!" Jay shouted.

"Help!" Petro called out of the barred window. "Help! He's crazy!"

"Help!" Eric cried next. "Help! OH JAY I'M SO SORRY!" he shouted, loud enough to be heard by everyone outside.

"Coming." Petro muttered as he saw the young guard slowly inching toward them. "Help please, our friend is bleeding internally!"

"You heard him." Eric mumbled to Jay. The young man quickly smeared some blood on the middle of his shirt and around the corners of his mouth and continued his wailing.

"What's going on in here?!" the guard demanded.

"Please, our friend. Eric attacked—"

"Don't lie, you…minx!" Eric shouted at him. "You came on to me first!"

"He's lying!" Petro said. "He hit on me and I told him to back off. Then he hit me."

"You hit me!"

"We hit each other."

"What happened to him?!" the guard shouted, looking at the clearly-mortally wounded Jay on the floor. Eric was hovering over him, pressing against his chest as if to stop his bleeding.

"Eric attacked me with a knife!"

"LIAR!" Eric shouted.

"Poor Jay was trying to stop him and…and…" Petro broke down into a sob.

"Oooh, oooh." Jay moaned.

"He's fading!" Eric shouted.

The guard looked left and right, clearly conflicted. "Back up!" he snapped as he fumbled for the keys to unlock the door. A moment later it creaked open and Petro leapt on top of him. Eric followed after, wrestling away the dagger the guard was already drawing and clocking him in the jaw. A second guard was already racing over, but Jay flew out of the carriage and tackled him before he could put a sword in Eric's back.

"Easy peasy. Get that carriage open." Eric said, tossing the ring of keys to Petro.

"For the record, my plan is better." he said as he unlocked Marcella's carriage.

"Give it up, we don't even **have** a wig." Marcella said as she hopped out, carrying little Dun in Fortigo's bag. The quadriplegic mute looked more put-out and bored than anything.

"Where's Fortigo?" Eric asked, jogging over to check on the rest of his party.

"They took him inside. Sal too." Marcella replied, pointing with her thumb to the Inn behind her. "The Inquisitor's gone up the road, though."

"What's up the road?" Jay wondered, looking back to the path that leads over a hillside.

"The rest of town." Marcella replied. Eric was already walking away from them, toward a row of horses that were tethered to the side of the Inn.

THE LADY IN THE LAKE

"Where are you going? We have to get Fortigo?" Marcella shouted as Eric untied a horse and climbed up.

"You all get him. Meet me when you do." Without a second word, Eric tore away from them, galloping his horse as fast as it could go.

"Wait—" she started to reply, but he was gone.

"I'll go with him." Petro said. "You and Jay get Fortigo and meet us in town."

"Be careful." Marcella said sincerely.

"Don't worry. I have a plan!" he said with a snap of his reins.

*****

"Okay, you got this." Petro said as he talked with himself. "It's no big deal. You're just coming out is all. You almost did it in the carriage but it's fine. You're going to be fine. They won't judge you." His horse approached the rest of Grenoble, which rested on the bottom of a hill. His horse perched at the top looking down on the town. "This is fine. We're all different in our own ways. We're all special. Glass houses and throwing stones and all that. They won't—"

A stone hit him on his shoulder blade, nearly knocking him off his horse. "Get down!" Eric whispered. Petro turned to see his black head barely peeking out of a bush off the road.

"Aren't we going into town?" Petro said stepping into the tall bushes and lying on his belly next to Eric.

"Not yet. I want to see what he's doing." He looked behind them for a moment, but nothing came into view. "That was quick; where are the rest?"

"Still back there. I left them to come help you."

"I don't need help." Eric said coldly.

"You need all the help you can get." He let Eric stare a hole into him for a moment and only spoke again after he looked away: "You haven't had time to grieve—"

"Not now, Petro."

"No, I'm serious. Holding things like that in is not good for the health. You need to talk things out, figure out what—"

"Not now, be quiet!" he snapped, nodding toward the town below as a fancy-dressed man exited a building to greet the Inquisitor. "Town Magistrate?"

"That's a fair guess...do you have a plan?" Petro asked.

"No."

"Well I do." Petro said, taking in a deep breath as though he had a big speech to unload.

"Wait, no I just thought of one." Eric said, interrupting Petro and hopping to his feet.

"Yeah but—" It was too late to protest; Eric

THE LADY IN THE LAKE

was halfway down the hill, sword drawn as he approached the building the Inquisitor and Magistrate had just entered.

Petro leapt to his feet and stopped halfway between the downward slope and his horse, wondering which would be faster, to mount the horse and head down after Eric or just run after him. After a few precious seconds of internal debate he decided to run. Then stopped after a few feet and turned back to get his horse, figuring—rightly so—one can never know when a horse might be needed.

By the time he burst into the building, Eric had the Inquisitor on the floor, sword pressed against his throat, screaming like a mad man about burning him alive or stoning him to death. "This was your plan?"

"It worked, didn't it." he said to Petro before turning back to the Inquisitor, who was nothing like the calm and collected man they'd met earlier. "Didn't it?"

"What do you want? My pardon? I'll give it to y—ack!" The Inquisitor gasped and winced as Eric's sword pressed a bit more tightly around his adam's apple.

Petro backed up to the doorway and peered outside. "The rest should be along soon." he said, but Eric wasn't listening.

"What about you?" Eric shouted to the Inquisitor. "You working with him?"

"N-n-no, not a bit." the man replied.

"You just swore allegiance to the Emperor!" the Inquisitor squeaked from behind the sword.

"Well you threatened to burn down our town!"

"And I will!"

"No you won't." Eric said, ending the argument. "Take off your clothes."

"What?"

"Did I stutter? Take it off. Your stupid red on darker red striped pajamas."

"I don't have anything on under this."

"Would you rather be naked or dead?" Eric lifted himself off the Inquisitor so he could stand and disrobe.

"Someone will have to untie me in the back...I'm serious. I usually have a servant do this."

With a roll of his eyes, Eric motioned for the Magistrate to do the deed. A moment later the three small knot that secured the Inquisitor's tunic were undone and he slipped it off along with his cloak and pants. He held his garments in his hands, looking small and pathetic. Whether that was the purpose for Eric's command or just a happy side-effect was not yet clear.

"What are you going to do with my clothes?" he mumbled.

"I'm going to wrap them around a scarecrow and hang them in effigy." Eric said, stone-faced.

"Seriously?" Petro asked.

"No. I'm going to sneak into Vatican City and kill the Emperor."

"You're insane." the naked man said. "Are you going to kill me too?"

"Yeah, probably." was all Eric said in reply. A muffled shouting from outside grabbed all their attention. Petro ran back to the door to check. "It's them...oh merde." he cursed.

"What?"

"They're bringing company."

Eric looked to the Magistrate, whose eyes were everywhere by on the Inquisitor. He noticed Eric's gaze and cleared his throat. "I'm wondering how to politely ask everyone to please leave our town."

"Do you have a sword?"

"Yes."

"Get it. And don't let this one leave...or get dressed." Outside, Eric and Petro ran to the center of the road, watching as the rest of their party raced toward them on horseback, chased by Templar in hot pursuit. "Did they not kill **any** of them when they rescued Fortigo?" he asked, exasperated at the overwhelming odds against them.

"You really want to kill the Pope?" Petro asked him, sounding way too calm than he should have as a dozen Templar rode toward them.

"I want to kill the Emperor."

"You're going to need help."

"Yeah well I was hoping I wouldn't have to ask."

"I don't mean from us. You know we'll help you." Petro said, watching the horses kicking up a cloud of dust in their wake.

"Who else you have in mind?"

"The Lady who lives in the Lake. She's the sister to Morgana, who is controlling the Roman Emperor."

"How do you know that?"

Petro didn't answer. Instead he stepped forward and stretched his arms out in either direction. The ground under Eric's feet trembled slightly. A ripple slid under him, nearly knocking him over. He watched as it stretched under the earth and rolled toward the approaching horsemen.

"Watch out for ours—" Eric started to say, but just as he did the ripple disappeared, sinking deeper into the dirt before exploding out of the ground and consuming the Templar in a whirlwind of dirt and rock. A few moments later Marcella and the rest trotted to them, each wearing a face of utter shock and bewilderment.

"Do you have Fortigo's bracelets?" she asked. Petro shook his head and allowed a wry smile to cross his face.

"Told you I had a plan."

THE LADY IN THE LAKE

"Why didn't you do that before…or anytime before right now?!"

"I'm…an ex-conjurer." he said, blushing a bit. "It's not really safe to talk about."

"Do you know Merlin?" Eric asked him, suddenly filled with a million questions.

"I know **of** Merlin…and his sisters of course. We all know about them."

"Why do you think she can help us? The Lady."

"She has been fighting against her sister for…I don't even know how long. She's been working behind the scenes to slow her, distract her, whatever she had to do to stop her from fulfilling her quest."

"What is her quest?"

"She wants the world." Petro shrugged. "But The Lady has the key to stopping her under the Lake. You want to kill the Pope, you're going to have to go through Morgana."

"Wait, you want to kill the Pope?" Marcella asked.

"What's the key?" Eric asked.

"A sword. Supposedly unbeatable, it was made with Morgana's power. The Lady's been keeping it hidden for years."

"Excalibur." Eric said. "She has it?" Petro nodded. "Take me to her."

"What do I do about the naked man?" the Magistrate shouted. The Inquisitor was standing in front of him sword pointed at his back while he continued holding his clothes against his naked body.

"Geez, Eric, what did you do while we were away?" Marcella asked.

"You have a jail. Use it."

"They may come looking for him."

Eric looked at the pathetic naked man. "Well? How many know you're here? How many will be coming for you?"

"None. I handle my own business."

"There you go. Put an old tunic on him—something itchy—and lock him up."

"Wait!" the Inquisitor said. "I don't want to spend the rest of my life rotting in some dingy cell…You said you would kill me!"

"I lied." he said, before turning to Marcella. "What about Sal?"

She shook her head as a look of contempt curled on her lip. "Took off after we broke Fortigo out. Stole a horse and rode away from town."

"Alright. That's something for later…" he turned to Fortigo. "You okay?"

"Oh sure, I'm great. They just wanted to ask me about if there were any more of us or if we'd think about bending the knee to the Emperor. Then they hit me and stuff."

"You're a tough one, my friend."

"All I thought the whole time they had me was how I had to get back to my little buddy."

THE LADY IN THE LAKE

Fortigo swung Dun around in his bag, holding it out in front of him. All the little man could do was rub his cheek against the golden bracelets the giant was wearing. "Aww, he's nudging me like a kitty."

"Are you ready?" Petro asked.

"For what?" Eric replied, wondering about the odd look in his companion's eyes. Petro stretched out his hands again and this time, instead of a rumble under the ground there was a sinking feeling in their stomachs. Their surroundings melted away and they travelled through time and space, touching down on a very different place from which they'd just been standing.

MATTHEW L. MARTIN
CHAPTER 13 : A TURKISH WHIRLWIND

A vast body of water stretched out beyond them. Merlin and Rumpel stood on the shore watching the blue waves roll and stir as the wind whipped around them. "She'll be this way. Merlin said, looking out at the empty blanket of water that stretched as far as they could see.

"What, on the other side of the sea?" Rumpel said, his voice cracked and his eyes still bloodshot.

"There's an island…" Merlin said, looking down at his companion. "Are you up for this?"

"Yes. Your sister will help you and then she'll help me."

THE LADY IN THE LAKE

"Oh? I don't believe I promised that."

"You said she could help. She'll help."

"Well let's not quibble over the details right now. Let's just get to her." Merlin raised his hand and waved someone over. Rumpel turned around to see who it was but there was no one and nothing to see, other than the water.

"Uh…who—" he began to ask, but stopped at the sight of something rising from the waves. The mast of a ship lifted higher and higher as the vessel underneath ascended to the surface of the water. "Where's the rest of it?" he asked as it approached. All told, it wasn't much to look at. It had space enough for the two of them and a single black sail but it was hardly a glamorous thing.

"What were you expecting?" Merlin asked as he stepped toward the boat, walking on the water with a pitter-patter of splashing pellets.

"I was expecting something a little more dramatic, considering you had this thing hiding under the water. Something as impressive as that deserves a ship equally as impressive, don't you think?"

"I suppose, but it's not my ship. It comes and goes as needed and right now it's only needed for two." He held out an inviting hand and Rumpel joined him on board. Despite a strong wind blowing into their faces, the boat launched forward, slicing through the wind and waves toward the water beyond. "Say goodbye to

Portugal…or what will one day **be** Portugal."

"What is this sea we're on?" Rumpel said, observing the turbulent waves.

"This is not a sea. This is the ocean…but we'll be meeting the Sea soon. My sister's house is under the Great Sea…sort of. It's complicated."

"Complicated or not, so long as this boat gets us there in one peace, I'm happy."

"Oh this boat has carried many needed travelers to see The Lady in the Lake. It's done its job for generations."

"Lady in the Sea you mean."

"Do I?"

*****

Other than Merlin humming some tune and Rumpel stirring and refusing to sleep, the next hour passed in silence and uneventfulness. The silence ended with Rumpel shaking Merlin's arm with one hand and pointing to…something… with the other. "What is that?" he said, more than a little panicked.

"That's the Sea." Merlin said. Ahead of them was a band of blue so rich and so vibrant it made the waters they were currently traversing look dull and lifeless in comparison. The Great Sea pressed into the Ocean and it into the Sea, creating a natural dividing-line of remarkable beauty. "Look. The path between the water." Merlin said as though that was a thing Rumpel should have

THE LADY IN THE LAKE

known about. The small man turned his head in the direction of Merlin's pointing, to see a lonely grey peak appearing through the fog ahead of them. "That's where we're going."

"I thought you said your sister lived on the Sea."

"This is the Sea." Merlin replied, as their boat crossed over the dividing line into the Great Sea. "And her home is only accessible by boat, unless you have something like one of these." he added, holding up his magic wand.

"I see...and what's that?" Rumpel asked, pointing behind them.

"That's where the Sea meets the Ocean. We just talked about that."

"No...what's **that**?"

Merlin turned around to see, hovering over the water, a twisting whirlwind of blue, a mixture of sea and ocean, lingering behind them ominously. "I don't know what that is..." he confessed.

Dark clouds formed overhead, seemingly materializing out of nowhere. Seconds later ran began to pelt them from above, drowning their hearing and slowly filling up around them. The whirlwind inched forward, like a thick waterspout, spitting water and unnatural gusts of wind that threatened to capsize their boat. A shape appeared in the center of the vortex, the singular figure of a woman, hovering over the water, controlling the storm.

"It's her." Rumpel muttered.

It was. MadSu approached, face full of fury, holding Merkal's staff with vengeance on her mind. "It's going to be okay. We have her right where we want her."

"We do?"

"We do."

"And where is that?"

"Right here." Merlin said before disappearing.

Left alone, Rumpel grabbed hold of one side of the boat, as the approaching whirlwind stirred the waters around him. "You leave me be!" he shouted at the storm. "I've paid for my crimes!"

A voice rumbled out of the swirling mass of wind and water: "My gold, my land, my oath."

"The gold is gone; it's not coming back. I will leave you land for good, too!"

"My oath." she repeated.

"What oath? I don't know anything about any—"

"Back!" Merlin's voice popped in beside him and a second later his body joined them. "Sorry it took some convincing."

"What did?"

"This did!" he shouted, holding his arms out to present… whatever it was he thought was about to happen.

THE LADY IN THE LAKE

Nothing happened though.

Even MadSu had held her place, preparing herself for whatever the wizard had conjured. "Maybe, if you can just disappear like that, you could just grab me and just whisk us over to your sister's house from here?"

"I told you this boat's the only way in or out of her house. Just wait. It'll happen."

"What will happen?" Rumpel asked, frustrated.

"Just...wait!" And then, as if on cue, the water around MadSu's whirlwind began to ripple. "There it is." the old wizard said. The water began to bubble, like a cauldron that was seconds away from spilling over. "Here it comes, oh you are not ready for this!" he taunted. The water was at a fervor now, ready to blow. MadSu's expression had grown from curiosity to boredom, however. Even Rumpel seemed put-out.

Then the water settled and all was calm.

"Oh come on!" Merlin cried.

"Just do something else!" Rumpel shouted.

"You might be the worst wizard I've ever killed." MadSu barked at him.

"You haven't killed me yeOH THERE IT IS!" Merlin shouted, just as a creature burst out of the water, right behind the whirlwind. It peaked in the sky, revealing the fullness of its tan and white serpentine body, before it turned down toward MadSu, its mouth opened wide to consume its prey.

The would-be witch stared in disbelief at the creature descending upon her, the creature from her own legends and myths, somehow here, back from the dead and far from the sand. The serpent crashed into the whirlwind, swallowing her whole before crashing back into the Sea. It surfaced a few seconds later, taking to the air again as Merlin flicked his wand at it. With a *BANG* and a burst of purple smoke, Archimedes belly flopped into the water.

"Oop, sorry! Bad aim!" Merlin shouted before twisting his wand again at the Sea. The dark cloud and rain had already dissipated but a new whirlwind, calmer and smaller than MadSu's twisted into shape, carrying Archimedes wet and worn out body over to their boat. The old man rolled into the cramped ship, huffing as much out of annoyance as he was tiredness.

"You can't keep doing this to me." Archimedes groaned.

"Sure I can." Merlin said with a happy smile. "Besides, you said you wanted to meet my sister."

"I meant around a table, with drinks and a game of rummikub."

"Don't be silly old boy. Look, we're almost there." he said, pointing to the quickly-

THE LADY IN THE LAKE

approaching spire. There was no dock ahead of them, no gentle beach on which to rest. There was just a wall of rock, quickly approaching. Rumpel grabbed the side of the ship once more, and Archimedes took the other side. Merlin remained in the middle, perfectly still, happy and content.

The ship began to descend.

"You both might want to hold your breath. Just for a second."

"I can't swim…" Rumpel blurted out.

"Neither can I!" Merlin said happily. "Isn't that funny? I've been walking on water ever since I got here. I guess I never saw the blubblubblubblub." Bubbles popped out of his mouth as he tried to speak underwater. The whole vessel was submerged and for a moment all they could see was the dull blue of the Sea beneath them.

After a moment, whether it was because their eyes adjusted to the darkness and the water, or if there was some magic playing a part, Rumpel and Archimedes did not know; what they **did** know was that something was coming into focus below them: small orange lights, flickering almost like candlelight. The deeper they descended they more vivid the lights grew until finally, with a rush of air that smacked them in the face and caused them to gasp, the trio inhaled and wiped the water off their face.

MATTHEW L. MARTIN

Before them was a glistening city, filled with buildings tall and small, each dotted by lanterns that hung from window seals and awnings. The Seabed was its main-street, running a wide path through the center of the town and branching off down alleys. Apart from being under water it was exactly what you'd expect a city of the era to be.

"Well that and the dearth of people." Merlin said, correcting the narrator.

"Where **are** the people?" Rumpel asked.

"Gone. All but The Lady remains. The rest are…yonder."

They moved effortless through the city, floating on air as though it were water, passing building after building, each of them abandoned and lifeless but for the torchlights that all continued to shine. The road curved away and the buildings grew more scarce, after a while there was nothing around but phosphorescent trees that shimmered with reds, blues, greens and yellows.

"It's beautiful…" Archimedes mumbled, which is shocking because he was not often one to offer up a compliment without being prompted.

"It was once." Merlin said, his happy smile fading a tad. "I grew up here. I was born in that building back—" He stopped as he turned around, furrowed his brow and stared intently at nothing behind them.

"What is it?" Rumpel asked.

"Nothing. I thought I saw movement, which

would be quite unusual…anyway, yes this was my home until I was old enough to leave it."

The small boat glided through the glowing forest before reaching what looked like a tear in a painting…if the environment around them were a canvass, that is. Cracked, crooked and stretching forever in both directions, it might've been a river had it been crystal-blue; instead it was pearly white and shining with the same phosphorescence as the forest behind them.

"It **is** a lake." Merlin said, answering the question on everyone's mind. "We call it Pelleas." The ship continued onward, crossing the pearly river to the other side. There, rising high above them, was a tall house, four stories high, with balconies, little round windows, a porch that wrapped around the whole of it and—like all the rest—a lantern hanging from the awning over the front door.

"Is this it?" Rumpel asked.

"Yes. This was our home…just her home now, I suppose."

"You lived here?" Archimedes asked, craning his neck to take in the massive structure. The size of it looked big enough to accommodate a family of twenty. "How many siblings did you have?"

"Several, I think. A lot of them only stayed with us for a short time. Foster took care of all her children, though only a few of us stayed for the duration. Me and my sisters."

"The duration of what?"

He didn't answer that question except with a smile. Instead, out of the boat he climbed, climbed up the steps and stepped to the front door. A great bronze knocker was placed at eye-level to Rumpel; tall enough for a child to reach it. "Go ahead, then." Merlin said to the little man. Rumpel knocked twice on the door, which opened immediately.

"There's no one home." Rumpel said as he stepped in side. The doorway opened to a vast sitting room, stretching two stories high, with a lifeless fireplace on one end, and several cushy chairs on the other. In between was a long, rectangular rug with a pattern of stars, moons and suns etched into the fabric. There were no lights burning inside and cobwebs stretched across all corners.

"It's me…" Merlin said loudly. "I am a friend." he added, before rolling his eyes. "I am a **brother**, sorry, wrong house."

"Brother." a voice responded. Soft and sweet, it fluttered through the air like a feather in the wind, resting in Merlin's right ear. "It's been a long time." she said.

"I wouldn't have come if things had not gotten so bad."

"How bad have things gotten?" her voice asked.

THE LADY IN THE LAKE

"Bad enough. It feels like she's ready to make her move. We've also encountered a staff-wielder in the Turkish lands."

"Oh? Is she on your side or your sister's?"

"Neither I think. She's a wild one but she's been dealt with, I think."

"You think?" Rumpel piped in, a bit of shock in his tone.

"It doesn't matter now. What matters is it's time. You told me when the time came you'd act. You told me you'd bring him back."

"...Arthur." the voice replied.

"Yes." Merlin said, his head hanging low. "And I'm sorry we fought and I'm sorry I was impatient. Nevertheless the time **has** come. It may not have been time then but it is time now. You must go and bring him back. I can not go there."

"Arthur was brought back. Not too many months ago."

Merlin expelled a relieved sigh. "Excellent news. Where is he?"

"They took him to your house in France. They thought that would be a safe place, away from...emerald eyes. Somewhere they could prepare him for the fight ahead."

"Who is they?" Archimedes blurted out.

"The librarian, the seraph and our sister." the voice answered, changing slightly with every word. By the time she finished speaking it was an entirely different person's voice, richer and louder than how The Lady usually spoke. It was foreign to Rumpel and Archimedes but Merlin recognized it immediately.

"Show yourself." he said flatly.

A pair of green eyes appeared in front of them, standing in the doorway that led to the dining room of the house. A pale face formed around the emerald orbs, following by hair of raven-black and a dress to match. "Hello brother." Morgana said simply.

"Where is she?"

"In the lake."

"Stop playing games." he said sternly.

"I'm not. She's in the lake." the door behind them swung open and they spun around to see The Lady, frozen inside a large crystal. It hovered over the lake, dripping glowing water before dropping back in with a splash of pearly white. In its place was a figure that was approaching from behind: A woman sitting atop a whirlwind, staff in hand.

"Impossible." Archimedes balked. "I swallowed her up."

"I thought I saw her following us..." Merlin said before turning back to his sister; Morgana was watching MadSu approach with a mystified look. "Morgana, this is MadSu, the guardian killer." he said, stepping aside and pulling his two companions away with him.

MadSu's whirlwind crashed through the

THE LADY IN THE LAKE

front doors as the tip of her staff radiated with a yellow glow, illuminating the room around them. "You are the witch that plagues the Old Lands? The one who wants to rule the world?"

"That's the short of it, yes." Morgana said. "Who are you again?"

"Your judge and executioner!" she shouted, thrusting her staff toward the raven-haired witch. A spark of yellow burst from the tip...but that's about it.

"Your gavel's broken, judge..." Morgana said. MadSu looked fiercely at her, then tried whatever she was trying the first time a second time; nothing happened again. There weren't even sparks this time. "Your staff." Morgana tried again. "It's cracked. You were lucky to have enough juice in it to get down here."

"ARGH!" MadSu shouted, charging for Morgana with a drunken rage. Whether she planned on pelting her with the stick like a blunt weapon or perhaps draw a dagger and try and stab the witch to death, it didn't matter: Morgana opened her mouth like an unholy angler fish and swallowed her whole.

"She'll be back." Archimedes snapped. "I did the same thing, just so you know. She'll be back."

"Where is Arthur?" Merlin demanded.

"I cut him into a hundred little pieces...with this." she said, holding up her hand revealing

Excalibur's ruby hilt wrapped around her fingers. "And then I exploded those hundred into a million little pieces," she added with a shrug, "until there was none of him left. Was that the hero you thought would beat me? The descendant of Avalon? Of my Tomas? With my own sword? You really are a terrible planner."

Merlin stepped forward but stopped suddenly as the rainbow blade of Excalibur was pointed at him. Morgana's other hand was held open, revealing a shimmering orange ring on her first finger. She hovered her palm over Merkall's staff on the ground below her. "What then?" Merlin asked. "Ride the Roman army to conquer the world?"

"Maybe...but unlike you I have more than one plan cooking at a time." Done talking, she drew her two hands together, touching staff to sword. Both they and the ring on her hand began to glow. The room around then shook as well. "I never liked this place. Foster never liked me, either."

"That's not true." Merlin said, stepping forward again. He was stretching an empty hand out toward her, keeping his wand in his other, concealed under his sleeve.

"Don't even." Morgana said. Her hands were shaking, trying to maintain a hold on three magical objects in her hands. "This house was filled with your happy memories. Yours and hers,

THE LADY IN THE LAKE

not mine. And not any of the others…and I'm through talking about it."

She slammed the staff into the ground, sending a shockwave of magic rippling away from it, knocking Merlin and his companions backwards. The staff split, running a crack from the bottom to the top and shattering like glass in her hands. "No bother." Morgana said as a portal opened behind her. "I have enough to do what I've always wanted to do…."

"And what's that." Merlin said, squeezing his wand tight in his hand, seconds away from using it…waiting for just the right opening; a sideways glance, a relaxed shoulder, anything to give him a chance…

"Send you to Hell where you belong." she said, darting her eyes to the floor under Merlin's feet. He had his opening and he took it, thrusting his wand forward and casting a spell just as the room around him melted away. He felt the bottom disappear out from under him and as he fell he looked up, seeing the circular-glow of the portal he'd fallen through.

He landed with a thud on a barren, rocky wasteland. Everything around was a dingy yellow and red, even the sky was a dark burgundy. A dry dull air filled his lungs and scratched his throat. Merlin picked himself up and examined his surroundings; not a soul was around, which surprised him more than a little. "This will take some cleverness…" he said to himself, looking up to the dark sky to see the tiny golden ring of Morgana's portal blink into nothingness.

"She screwed you too, eh?" a man behind him spoke. Merlin turned to see the only other living soul around, a man immaculately dressed in a burgundy and black.

"Who?" Merlin asked.

"Morgana. She and that boyfriend of hers."

"Are you…?"

The man simply nodded.

"Oh…merde." Merlin cursed, looking around again with a newfound realization.

"No, it's worse. It's Hell…and they took my army."

THE LADY IN THE LAKE

CHAPTER 14 : SECOND-BORN

Her fingers wrapped around the iron handle that secured the door and kept them out of sight from anyone who might be patrolling Camelot's courtyard. Gwen was hesitant, knowing what she needed to do and knowing she needed to project supreme confidence in her plan, while having little confidence it would actually work.

"What do you see?" Sir Richard asked, no doubt wondering what the delay was.

Mordred squeezed by his mother to peer out the small window cut into the door. "I don't see any one."

"Scouts on the wall?" Richard asked.

THE LADY IN THE LAKE

"No…it's strange, there are usually a dozen or so people moving here and there, especially this time of day."

"Baudwin has either sent them away to be replaced by more loyal men or they have left on their own. Either way we have a very small window of time to act. Gwen?"

"I'm ready." she said, staring directly across from them. Camelot's courtyard contained what most Castles of the day had: There were stable houses and farms, apartments on the wall for the servants and guards that patrolled (or were supposed to be) the wall and gatehouse. What set it apart from other castles was an addition Gwen personally oversaw over a decade earlier. A whole corner of the wall was demolished and rebuilt to accommodate a large covered crypt, capable of holding Kilgara, her second-born child.

"If you were ready we'd be there by now." Mordred said, reaching for the door handle himself to open their way if Gwen would not do it. She pushed his hand away, however.

"I **am** ready. I'm just…thinking about how he will react to seeing me."

"You?" Mordred scoffed. "He loves you. It's me he always hated."

"Yes but you didn't send him to rot in that dark place. You didn't see the look in his eyes when I locked him in."

"If it was the same look he gave me when he

nearly killed me, then yeah I've seen it a time or two."

"You were both just children. Neither of you knew better."

"Don't make excuses for him. Not again." Mordred snapped. At this point all pretense had been dropped. No one was leaving the dungeon stairway till mother and son worked out their issue.

"I'm not excusing him; I'm explaining why he did what he did. I am not excusing him." Gwen said again, as she often did to Mordred, knowing he sometimes needed short and simple statements to understand what was being said to him. "I sent him away, didn't I?"

"No, you didn't. You sent him to the crypt, not away. He should have been sent to Wales, where he could stretch out and live away from us."

"You don't understand. You're a child, not a parent." She shook her head, too frustrated to say all she wanted to say. "I don't know why you're so determined to hold this over my head. I chose you, didn't I? You over him."

"Well I was first-born, and he can't exactly be King can he? It had to be me."

"This isn't about your stupid crown." Gwen spat. "It was never about that." she added as she turned the handle and opened the door. The courtyard remained deserted. To their right, the

THE LADY IN THE LAKE

long line of storage buildings sat unguarded along the right wall. The tall residence towers of the King rose from their place against the northern wall, but there were no heads of soldiers peeking through the battlements on top. Even the gatehouse on the southern end of the compound—the only way in or out of Camelot—appeared deserted.

"They didn't all leave, surely." Mordred said, looking around.

"Perhaps the rank and file have more loyalty to you than you might think." Sir Richard said. "The rebellious Lords and Sir Baudwin are likely inside the Hall. The rest may be waiting to meet us…to fight back."

"Loyalty to my father, if anything." Mordred said bitterly. "Not loyalty to me."

Gwen jerked at the words of Mordred, startled to hear him say "my father." It was only a momentary reaction and she quickly recovered. *Arthur*, she thought to herself, *stupid woman, he means Arthur, not—*

"The way is clear." Richard said. "It may not be for long. Hurry."

They moved quickly across the southern end of the courtyard. As they passed the gatehouse, however, Richard grabbed Mordred and held him back. "Let her go alone; we need to be ready to open the gate."

"You can open the gate." Mordred said. There was a look in Richard's eyes that Mordred had missed, but Gwen noticed it as she turned around to listen to their conversation. Richard didn't want Mordred and Kilgara in the same confined place if he could help it.

"No, you help Richard. I'll be right back." she said and turned away, not waiting for a response. The door to the crypt was, like the dungeon, a plain iron gate. Unlike the dungeon there was no window to peer in or out of, meaning Gwen approached the door completely ignorant to the half-dozen guards, along with Lord Lot, that were just on the other side.

"Queen Gwenevere?" Lot said, turning around as the door opened. His face revealed surprise; this was no ambush. "Hold her." he said quickly. One of the soldiers grabbed her wrist and pulled her the rest of the way inside, shutting the door behind them, leaving Mordred and Richard unawares.

They were standing in a small square room with a door in the center of every wall. To her left and right were guards stepping out of rooms carrying bundles of food, grain from the room on the right and raw meat from the room on the left. Across from Gwen was the fourth door, reinforced with three iron rods that stretched horizontally across the gate. A chain was woven between them, synched together by a large round lock.

"How funny." Lot said. "We were just about to visit your other son. I take it you all have

THE LADY IN THE LAKE

escaped?"

"Just me." Gwen lied. The instant smirk on Lot's face let her know he didn't believe her for a second.

"When was the last time you were in this room? I'm told it's not a place you frequent." Lot waited for an answer but one did not come. What **was** heard, however, was the rattling of chains from the other side of the reinforced door. A muffled moan also reverberated around them. "You think that's hunger pains? How often is he fed?"

"Three times a day." Gwen answered stiffly.

"I see. I guess the amount has gone up over the years. That's a lot of meat to go through."

"No." Gwen said bluntly, before she could catch herself.

"No? You mean you're still feeding it the same amount all these years?" She did not answer, but that was answer enough for Lot. "At this point you're probably starving the poor thing." He turned to the soldier to his left. "Get another bundle of meat. Let's make a good first impression."

"What are you going to do?" Gwen asked, unable to suppress the anxiety in her tone.

"What your foolish son—your first one I mean—refused to do. I'm going to solidify my hold on this kingdom and… what was his name? Kilgara is it? He's going to help me."

"He won't help you. He's more likely to kill you." Gwen said the words, but she didn't quite believe them. Truth be told, Lot probably had a winning plan.

"If you really thought so you wouldn't have warned me, now would you?" She didn't answer but his smile widened all the same. "Take her back to her cell. I would say watch out for Mordred and Sir Richard but..." He chortled a bit. "What can they really do?"

Dragging her outside, Lot found the answer to his question. Mordred and Richard burst out of the gatehouse, swinging their stolen swords with everything they had. Unfortunately the weak young man and the weary old man were little match for the hardened soldiers. They were beaten up and knocked down, and though Gwen managed to shrug off one guard, she failed to take the other two, who drove their fists into her stomach with little regard. And then, just for good measure, they kicked her in the face, blacking her eye and knocking her out.

*****

She came to later in the evening, back in the cell she'd previously escaped from. Richard and Mordred woke her up. From the sound of it, they were in the cell opposite her, had just woke up themselves and were in the midst of a heated argument.

THE LADY IN THE LAKE

"I could have if you'd let me go!" Mordred was yelling.

"And done what? What would you have done? There were eight of them at least. Probably more."

"I am the King!"

"No. You are not. Baudwin is the King now. Right or wrong, fair or otherwise, he has the power not you."

"You shouldn't have kept me in the gatehouse." Mordred said, with the kind of tone that told Gwen he'd said that once already and was returning back to it in the middle of the argument.

"You're not thinking." Richard said bluntly.

"I'm not stupid!" Mordred shouted, sounding very much like an oversized child.

"I never said you were. I—look, you need to consider…" He sighed.

"What?"

"You need to think about other ways to win a fight… besides **fighting** I mean."

"You mean run away."

"That's one thing, yes."

"That's your skill Sir Richard, not mine."

"Watch it." Gwen said, sitting up with a grimace and staring disapprovingly at her son.

"How are you?" Richard asked.

"Fine." she replied, wincing as she did. "As fine as you are I suppose."

"Best thing we can do is just sit tight and wait for an opening." Richard said. Gwen nodded. Mordred looked back and forth at both of them and then remembered something he had previously been told; something that he thought little of until that exact moment.

"Are you two in love?" he asked bluntly.

"What?" they both answered immediately, looking at him and not each other.

"Are you?"

"Where did you get that idea?" Gwen asked.

"I was told…it doesn't matter who. Does Sir Richard only advise me so closely because it keeps him close to you?"

Now they were looking at each other.

"Sorry to interrupt." Lot said, his eyes shimmering in the torchlight as he stood behind the dungeon room door, pressing his face close to the barred window. "And I mean that. If it wasn't urgent I'd love to stay and hear all about where Sir Richard has been sheathing his sword. I mean, I know all about Sir Lancelot, but…Sir Richard too?"

"What about Sir Lancelot?"

"You still haven't told him? You've had plenty of time."

"There is nothing to tell."

"Your daddy's not your daddy, boy-King." Lot said, as casually as one would reveal a sports result. "Arthur was, by all accounts a good man.

THE LADY IN THE LAKE

Mediocre King, but good man. Gwenevere here…she fell for another. And **another** too, it seems." he added, nodding to Richard. "I'm racking my brain trying to imagine what any of them have in common. They all seem so different."

"They all had more valor than you." Richard said. Gwen's head was hung. Mordred looked more confused than angry as thoughts ripped through his mind.

"Maybe. But I guess that streak will be broken too." Lot said, stepping out of sight for a moment. The door rattled and unlocked, opening to reveal Lot and a pair of guards. "Just her." he said, directing the guards to unlock Gwen's cell. "They others can stay and finish their argument."

"Where are you taking her?" Richard asked.

"To the chapel to be wed." Lot said sarcastically. Gwen was dragged out of her cell and out of the dungeon room with Lot behind them. He moved to shut the door but stopped to turn back. "Sorry I just realized that sounded a bit too sarcastic before. We really **are** going to the chapel to be wed. A King needs a bride and Gwen certainly gets around."

Behind him, Gwenevere thrashed and kicked, desperate to break away from her captors. She'd have clawed Lot's eyes out had she slipped free. She could not, however. "I want to speak to Baudwin." she said. It was her only play, she knew. *If I could just have a minute to talk with him, reason with him.*

"He's dead." Lot said, opening the door at the top of the stairs. Crickets filled the night air as Gwen tried in silence to process what she'd been told. "It's what he wanted... eventually I mean. I doubt he expected it would happen so soon. I think he envisioned dying in his bed five or ten years from now, peaceful and happy, a King who saved England or something wistful like that. Ah well."

They did not turn right toward the Great Hall, as Gwen expected them too. Instead they continued straight, once more toward the crypt where Kilgara was kept. "I'm not going to marry you." she said plainly. "Find a whore."

"I found one." he said, laughing at his own comment. "Who else has there been besides Lancelot and Richard? How many while Arthur was putting down the rebellion at Canterbury?"

Gwen jerked a hand free and managed to connect with a slap across his face. She took a forearm to the back for her trouble but it was worth it. "Arthur was gone. I thought he was dead." she said, flubbing a bit of the timeline and leaving out the more terrible details, but this was no time for absolute verity. "Richard came later." she added. "Much later."

"I'm sure he did. Many times." Lot said, again laughing at himself. He was positively euphoric. "Anyway, it's my turn. I'm to be

THE LADY IN THE LAKE

crowned by the end of the week and I need a proper Queen at my side."

They stopped at the gate leading into the crypt. "Are you expecting Kilgara to perform the ceremony?"

"No…" Lot replied, opening the door just as three men stepped out. Actually, only two of them stepped out; the third man was being carried, with tattered clothes and a bloody stump in place of a left leg. "I'm going to need a wedding gift from you a little early." he said, holding a hand toward the open door, allowing the guards to help Gwen inside.

The scene was much different from the previous time she'd been in this room: A large blood streak was smeared across the floor, from the reinforced door in front of them to the exit behind them. A few shell-shocked guards were standing around on either side, eyes wide and pupils pin-pricked. "What happened here?" she couldn't help but ask.

"Your son, apparently." Lot answered. "Here's the thing: We have a small army making their way south from Manchester. They'll be here before the end of the week. From what we've been told they're…possibly looking to challenge my claim to the throne."

"Well that makes sense, considering you don't have one."

"I'm here aren't I? Finders keepers is a

pretty legitimate claim. The point is we don't have much of an army here, per say. What we have is scattered around, securing allegiance from Lords in the north and in the rest of Wales."

Now it was Gwen's turn to smile in amusement. Lot talked very much like a Lord's son; he was pampered and polished, with a silver tongue to match his immaculately polished armor, but he was still a novice to ruling. "You sent your army away?" Gwen asked, allowing her smile to widen.

"No. I sent some of them away. It was sound strategy."

"You fool." she chuckled. "You don't stage a hostile takeover and **then** send your muscle out to secure it. You organize your muscle first and then the takeover becomes a formality. They're going to kill you." she added with glee.

"Us. They're going to kill us if it comes to it. King and Queen."

"You'll be dead before the wedding…which I won't be partaking in willingly, I'll add."

"The fight will be over before it begins." Lot said, raising an overconfident correcting finger to the air. "Which is why we're here." With a nod to some nervous looking guards, the iron rods that held the reinforcement in place were removed and the heavy door creaked open.

A rush of stale, warm air nearly knocked everyone over. The door revealed only a barely-visible balcony overlooking a deep bowl cut into the earth. "I don't know what you expect me to do that you can't do yourself." Gwen said, peering over Lot's shoulder to the dimly-lit area beyond.

"I expect he will respond to his mother better than he responds to us."

"I wouldn't count on it." Gwen said, sounding confident but feeling uncertain.

"Let's find out." Lot said, handing over a heavy ring with one large, rusty key attached to it.

"What exactly do you want me to do? I'm not going to use him to fight a war for you."

"Just control him well enough for **us** to fight the war."

"Why would I do that? Why would I help you?"

"Because if you don't we'll kill your son and lover." Lot answered matter of factly.

He means it, Gwen thought. *If he'd kill his own father to take the throne on the first chance he had, he'd kill the former King to hold the throne without hesitation.* She would not be responsible, not even indirectly, for losing her first-born son. So, with a barely concealed grimace, she turned and entered the place where she'd kept her second-born son.

"My Lord, the prisoners want to talk to you." Gwen heard a guard tell Lot. She turned to respond to him, but the iron door slammed behind her, locking her in. She was either going to succeed or die; there was no middle ground. The air nearly choked her as she breathed it in, peering over the balcony to get a better look at the view.

If there was a bridge from one side to the other, it would stretch nearly a hundred feet across. There was no such bridge, however. There was no one brave enough or foolish enough to put their body over the center of the chasm. Torchlights—many of them either broken or extinguished—dotted the inner rings of the bowl, spiraling a dim light toward the center where…something was stirring, rattling chains as it did.

"I never thought I'd see you again." she said, listening as her words echoed around the room. The rattling chains fell silent. He was listening too. "I left you here because you were becoming a danger…to me, to Mordred, to yourself too probably: Welsh hunters would have taken you had I let you roam free. I have missed you, Kilgara—"

A rumbling rose from the depths of the pit, like a dog that growled to warn an approaching intruder to back off. Gwen did not back off, however. She walked the shallow path that twisted down to the center.

"I'm sorry you have been underfed. I only just thought of it…" She shook her head, angry at her own stupidity. "I never thought to tell the servants to feed you more as you grew. I can't imagine how thin and sick you must be." She

THE LADY IN THE LAKE

dared to pause her walking and stare down to the center. She could see his dark shape but the lights were all burned out down there, revealing nothing more than a barely-moving shadow. There was no way to tell how emaciated he was. *Too weak to fight*, she told herself. *They'll kill him when they realize...*

"I wonder..." she said as she continued her descent. "I wonder if you could forgive me, if not forever then at least for today..."

*****

"My Lord, the house servants have found King Baudwin." a cherry-clad soldier said, entering the outer room of the crypt as Lot remained by the iron door, waiting for his would-be bride and son-in-law to emerge.

"And?" Lot answered, barely interested.

"Nothing, they wanted me to tell you. They expect you will be issuing a statement and decreeing a week of mourning."

"That makes sense I suppose." Lot said, nodding. "But there's a wedding and a war to win. Send some servants to bury the old man. Make it a nice headstone too. Something for the peasants to admire when they visit his gr—"

BANG

The heavy iron door—barred once more as

soon as Gwen crossed beyond it—rumbled as something heavy crashed into it on the other side. While the soldiers and servants scurried backwards as fast as they could, Lot only smiled and casually stepped out into the courtyard.

BANG

The sound carried outside, where Lot and several brave spectators were waiting. "He might've killed her." one of the servants muttered to his companion.

BANG

"He might be too unruly to use." another servant whispered.

BANG

"Poor thing's been eating scraps for years. It's a wonder he's still aliv—"
"Enough." Lot said, his impatience growing. "Is he small enough to come out into the courtyard?" he asked.
"I'd think so, Lord…er, your highness?" the closest servant muttered.

BANG

"Good. Open the big door." Lot said, waving for a soldier to enter the crypt.

THE LADY IN THE LAKE

BANG

After a moment of hesitation, with the guard doing that thing where you silently point at yourself and mouth "me?" as if hoping he meant someone else (anyone else), the poor man entered and a moment later the ear-piercing screech of the iron rods being removed was heard in the courtyard.

CRASH

The door burst open and the guard who had just entered tried his best to scramble away. He was too slow however, Stumbling forward and being snatched by a pair of ruby jaws. Stepping out of the crypt was a red serpentine creature, with Gwen sitting atop him like a Knight would ride a horse.

Far from emaciated, Kilgara had thrived. Fifteen feet long, he stretched and twisted his neck as he chewed up and swallowed the guard, seemingly overjoyed to be freed from the heavy chains that had held him for so long. His eyes were milky white however, and he seemed to be seeing with his nose, sniffing in the air and snorting puffs of fire in equal measure.

"He's bigger than you thought, I assume?" Lot said. "He's bigger than **I** thought, at least." he added to himself, staring at the creature with envious eyes. "Send word to the Manchester army.

Tell them what we have and tell them to bend the knee." he said to an aid, who quickly turned to run.

"No." Gwen said, followed by a loud roar from the dragon she rode. The aid stopped in his tracks and turned to stare at the creature and his rider. "You leave my Castle. Now."

Lot did not flinch. "Bring me Mordred and his Knight." he said.

"Kill them and I will kill you." Gwen said. Kilgara seemed to read her thoughts; he stepped forward and lowered his head toward the Lord who would be King. "Every last one of you." she added as a faint glimmer of orange and red started to glow inside Kilgara's nostrils.

"Here!" the guard called, leading Mordred and Richard in front of him.

"Unchain them!" Gwen called.

"Do it." Lot said. "Now what? You expect me to just ride away?"

"Yes." Gwen replied. "Ride away, to the sea, and keep riding till the water is over your head."

"I surrender." Mordred said pathetically, but no one except Richard seemed to hear him.

"And what will you do?" Lot asked. "You've already been overthrown once. How many more like me do you think there are? The Scots and the Irish will march right to your front door if I leave."

"I surrender." Mordred said again, still to no

reaction.

"The Kingdom will unite around us once more." Gwen said.

"They will surrender to your enemies before you could even—"

"I surrender!" Mordred shouted, finally capturing the eyes of both Lot and Gwenevere. "I surrender. I'm done. You want the throne; take it."

"Be quiet." Gwen said.

"What's the plan, boy-King?" Lot asked, cocking his head sideways.

"No plan. I'm done with it all. I—no!" he shouted as Gwen and Kilgara reared back, ready to strike at the distracted Lot. Mordred grabbed the hilt of the guard next to him and drew the blade before anyone could stop him. Lot fell over but the beast did not get the chance to strike. Mordred lunged forward, driving the steel into the soft underbelly of his quasi-brother. The creature stumbled and flopped backwards, knocking Gwen to the ground as it did.

"Oh!" she shouted, at a loss for words. "What did you do?!" she cried, watching the dragon wheeze and snort meager puffs of smoke and sparks as blood pouring from its chest. "Why?" she asked as Mordred picked her up. Regret washed over her as she remembered the day he hatched, how she initially rejected him as a memory of the man who violated her, a memory she wanted to erase. He kept finding his way back to her, every night, slipping out of the stables, up the castle wall, through her window and into her bed, to nestle under her arm the way she had held his egg for months after returning to Camelot.

More memories slipped in and out of her mind but so did the thumping of the blood pounding in her head, a rage that boiled up inside her, blinding her to the fact that she was being dragged once again to a place she did not want to be: Away from her dying son. She shrugged Mordred off her and charged for Lot, only to be seized by Richard. "This was the only way." he said. "They're letting us go."

"Not me..." she said, shaking her head at how pointless all this hand been. "Just you and Mordred. This was all for nothing."

"No." Mordred said. "You're coming too."

"Seize her!" Lot shouted, still on the ground. "Seize all of them."

"You said—" Richard started, but Lot cut him off.

"You killed my weapon!" he shouted, pointing an accusing finger toward them. "My—"

Dying and barely conscious, Kilgara lunged, snapping his jaws at the sound of Lot's voice. His teeth sunk into flesh and clamped through bone, taking off the Lord's arm from the elbow down. He wailed and everyone rushed to drag him out of the creature's reach, giving Mordred and Richard time to snag a pair of horses and throw Gwen onto

THE LADY IN THE LAKE

one.

"No…" she mumbled, watching as the guards took turns driving swords into the weakened dragon's body. They were out of the gatehouse and down the road before she spoke again, asking her son "Where are we going that they won't hunt us and find us?"

"Germania." Mordred said. "Let them find us there if they want. They won't. They will stay here and rule and the one-armed King will be killed by Fenial or some other traitor. Either way, we'll be far from here."

"There's nothing in Germania. Not anymore." Gwen said.

"Exactly."

MATTHEW L. MARTIN
CHAPTER 15 : THE LADY AND THE LAKE

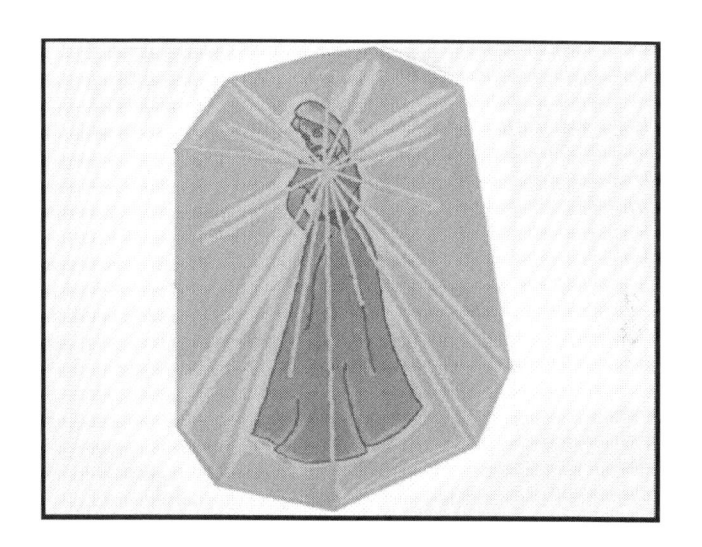

The six of them touched down on the beach, wind whipping around them. A storm was brewing; they could see it pouring over the water, not too far from where they were standing. Eric breathed in the salty air and looked around to try and determine where exactly they were. "Is this Rome?" he asked, a little worried that the answer was yes.

"No, it's the western part of Iberia." Petro said, untying the many knots that kept his long grey robe together. He let the fabric fall to the ground, revealing more traditional looking garments underneath. They, along with his now-

THE LADY IN THE LAKE

unkept hair, almost made him into an entirely new person.

"You could have dressed normal all this time?" Jay asked, in awe of the very different looking man standing next to him. "Why dress up like some peasant in a bathrobe?"

"It was important for me to look…not like I used to look."

"On the run, huh?" Jay asked, scrunching his face as he did, looking very much like a boy and not a wanted criminal.

"We're all on the run." Eric said, turning toward the group. "Only you're not just being hunted by Romans, are you?"

"Not exactly, no." Petro conceded.

"You're one of them." Marcella said. It wasn't a question. "You're a guardian, or a wizard or whatever."

"A magi." Eric said. "The guardians are a special class."

"Actually I **was** a guardian."

"What country?" Fortigo asked, stepping into the conversation with Dun sleeping in his backpack.

"Germania." Petro said. "I shepherded that kingdom years ago, but…I left." He twisted his hand in the air, rolling his fingers around like a gambler plays with dice. Sparks of red and purple popped and fizzled around his hand, like miniature fireworks conjured out of nothing. "I was not appreciated. I was **hated** actually. Truth be told I was never very good at what I did. I didn't even want to do it but they cast lots and I was chosen. I didn't last more than a year, if I recall." He looked around to their faces, trying to determine if and how they were judging his words. "There are others like me." he said, defensively. "Other guardians who have left their Kingdoms and who refused to sail to the skull islands. Others who just wanted to live here and enjoy life while they did it."

"What's a skull cave?" Jay asked. It was a reasonable question but the fact that he asked Fortigo was not the most sensible choice. Fortigo thump-thumped the little redhead's forehead as though the answer was obviously someone's giant head.

"It's the place where his people come from…" Eric answered, remembering simpler days serving the court of King Arthur and his Wizard counselor. "It's where guardians go back to when they're done on earth."

"All magi and conjurers and guardians alike, actually." Petro corrected him. "Anyone who comes from there or who learns the arts down here eventually returns to a skull island."

"Why?" Marcella asked. "Why not stay and retire?"

"Great power brings with it great accountability. If we aren't working with our powers we will likely end up abusing our powers. This world is not meant to have miracle workers here forever."

"I've been to a skull cave." Eric said suddenly.

"I know." Petro responded. When Eric looked at him with surprise, he added with a shrug: "I still get the memos."

"What exactly are you people?" Jay asked.

"Don't bother." Eric said before Petro could respond. "Merlin never explained it; Petro won't either."

Jay gave his companion a wishful look but only shook his head. "Truth be told my young friend, I don't even know what I am."

"Well what **do** you know?"

"I know our ride is here." Petro answered, pointing over Jay's shoulder toward the ocean. A small black sail was rising from the waters, eventually revealing a craft big enough to accommodate exactly six.

"Did you do that?" Fortigo asked, looking astounded.

"That? Oh no, that's just what happens when you want to visit The Lady. It's like Uber…or it **will** be." he said cryptically.

When the last person climbed into the boat, it lunged forward, turning toward its destination with neither wind nor oar to steer it. Minutes turned to hours with nothing but the ocean blue in front of them. "Is it far?" Marcella asked, trying her best not to sound impatient.

"Well it's…it's not far, no." Petro said, shifting his eyes left and right, looking far more uncertain than he had when they left.

"You do know where we're going, yes?" Eric asked.

"Yes, The Lady."

"Right…you do know how to get there?"

"Well no…of course I don't. The boat does, though. Just trust the boat." Petro's eyes kept darting around the water, as though he was expecting something to burst out of the waves at any moment. His anxiety lingered as their journey continued without incident.

After another two hours of no incident, the passengers were getting mighty restless. "We're lost." Fortigo said plainly.

"No we're not." Petro assured him, but his wandering eyes did not inspire confidence.

"Yeah we are. I know what lost looks like. I'm lost quite often. This is lost. We're lost."

"We're not lost we just…started farther away than I expected us to."

"What do you mean, where did you expect us to start?" Eric asked.

"Closer to the big rock where she lives. There must have been some activity near there, something that kicked us way back where we started, out of the way."

THE LADY IN THE LAKE

"Are you saying…what are you saying?"

"I'm saying The Lady knew we were coming but she didn't want us reaching her so quickly. I'm saying something must have happened."

"Do we keep going?" Jay asked.

"You say that like we have a choice." Eric replied. "Feel the wind? It's pushing against us yet we're slicing through it all the same. We're going where we're going, come what may.

*****

Another hour passed, then two. Finally Petro stirred, sitting up straight and pointing to a place where Ocean met sea. "We're almost there." he said, looking left and right.

"What is it?" Marcella asked, noticing his wandering gaze.

"Something happened here." he said, moving his finger in the air around the perimeter of water that seemed—to everyone else—to be perfectly normal.

"I don't see anything." Fortigo said, dipping his hand in the convergence of Ocean and Sea and letting the water slip through his fingers. "It's just water."

"There was a fight. This place has known magic."

"You know, we could have used all your crazy wizard skills for **years**." Eric said shaking his head and looking out to the Sea as their boat sailed ahead. "There's nothing here. What are you seeing?"

"I don't know exactly. I just know we need to keep our guard up." He stopped as though he was finished and then said the first thing that came to his head. "Merlin was here."

"And The Lady?" Eric asked.

"No...she's there." Petro said, pointing to the tall spire of a rock, rising from the southern edge of Iberia to their left. Just as Merlin and Rumpel had done previously, their boat slipped under the water and entered the city beneath the waves. They crossed the glowing, pearly river, which flowed under them so slowly and so peacefully it might as well have been a standing lake.

The Lady's house sat quietly in front of them. Other than the front door—which was swung open ominously—there was nothing remarkable about it. Nevertheless Petro was entirely on edge, constantly jerking his head around as if certain they were being watched. "Something is here, I'm sure of it." he mumbled.

"I should hope so." Eric said as he stepped in first through the doorway. Despite Petro's worries, however, no one was home. "Look around." he said, sending the rest of them fanning out in all directions. Eric and Marcella stepped into a spacious dining room, dark and stale, but not quite un-lived in.

THE LADY IN THE LAKE

"Weird." Marcella said.

"What is?"

"There's no one here, seems like no one has been here for a while, there's dust everywhere but there are smears and streaks all over the place."

"So someone was here, but not for long." Eric said, examining a tall china cabinet, filled with pearly white dishes with blue accents painted on them.

"Eric." a voice whispered in his ear. He spun around to see Marcella on the other end of the room, rummaging through a few books that were sitting on a small table.

"What?" he said aloud.

"What?" Marcella threw the question back at him.

"You said my na—"

"Outside." the voice whispered again.

"H—Hey!" Jay called. "There's something here!"

"Go." the voice said, nudging him forward. Marcella gave no indication she heard it but Eric couldn't deny it. He exited the room, left the house and jogged with Marcella toward Jay, who was standing at the edge of the glowing river.

"There's something in there." the young man said, peering over and staring into the water.

"A person?" Marcella asked.

"I don't think so…it's like a big rock."

"You called us out here for a rock?"

"It's not a rock." Eric said, looking into the river. He laid his belly down onto the wet ground and plunged his face into the water. He had expected it to be cold but instead he felt nothing. It didn't even feel like water. He did a stupid thing, opening his mouth to see if it would fill with liquid. Instead he inhaled pure, crisp air, just as he'd done when the boat dipped below the Sea.

Pressing his palms into the earth, Eric tried to lift his face and body up but something was preventing him. A second of panic came over him and he began to squirm, trying to break free from whatever had hold of him.

"Let go." the voice whispered.

For no good reason at all, Eric listened to the voice, opened his hands and slipped into the water. He fell slowly, floating, toward the object at the bed below. The rock—as Jay had called it—was far from an ordinary river stone. It was a shimmering crystal, easily six feet tall, glowing with an iridescent hue that reminded Eric immediately of the way Excalibur would sparkle with all the colors of the rainbow whenever Arthur wielded it.

The closer he got, the more he realized something was inside the stone. The figure of a woman turned and stared as he approached. Her lips moved and her head tilted but the voice Eric heard did not come from in front of him, distorted by the crystal between them; it slipped into

THE LADY IN THE LAKE

Arthur's ear as though she was pressed close against him.

"I was wrong about Arthur." she said.

"How?" Eric replied.

"I wanted him to be something he's not."

"I don't understand."

"This story needs a hero. I've known it for quite some time. Foolishly I tried to make Arthur the one to defeat my sister. That's not for him."

"What is for him? Isn't he dead?"

"He wasn't...then he was, now he's simply...away."

"Can you be a little less cryptic?"

"My sister wants to rule the world. What do you want?"

"Me? Who cares what I want?"

"The world does, believe it or not."

"...I don't know what I want."

"Yes you do. You want vengeance."

"How do you know?" Eric asked, knowing full well she was right on the money.

"I've seen your life. I know what you've suffered, how it's hardened you. I have something for you."

"Can't you get out of this?" Eric asked, rubbing his hand over the smooth surface of The Lady's confinement.

"Great magic put me here. Only great magic can free me."

"I have someone with me who might—"

"Cullich can't help me. He would do better entering a skull cave and fulfilling his mission."

It took Eric a moment before he realized who "Cullich" was. *Of course Petro would not be his real name…*

"Morgana and her sword put me here. Only it release me, but it doesn't matter. I'm not the hero of this story."

"Do you have the sword? The Librarian brought it to you, didn't he?"

"He did…but that was then. She has it now. So I'll ask you again: What do **you** want?"

"Vengeance." he admitted.

"I kind of want that too, but I think justice is a better word, don't you?"

"I guess." Eric said, not really believing it. "I'm no good to you, though."

"Why do you say that?"

"I know what you're doing, trying to draft me to lead your fight against your sister. I have my own fight to win."

"Your fight against Rome is my fight against Morgana. We share a common foe."

"Whatever. I am not interested in being the puppet of some lady in a crystal coffin or her crazy brother. I'm done with that life. Choose someone else."

"But **I** didn't choose you, Eric. You were chosen from the beginning and I was too distracted by Arthur's destiny to realize it."

THE LADY IN THE LAKE

"Well I officially unchoose myself, thanks." A moment of silence lingered between them, broken by Eric's impatient: "Can I go now?"

"You can go anytime you want." she said, and as if on cue, Eric found himself sitting on the river bank, still and calm as though he'd been sitting there peacefully for an hour.

"What happened?" Marcella asked him.

"It was a mistake coming here. She doesn't want to help us. She just wants us to help her."

"How do you know? Is she down there?"

"Yeah."

"No she's not." Fortigo said, pointing at the river as the multi-colored crystal emerged, hovering over the water. The Lady remained inside, looking at them equally beautiful and sad.

"Come on, everyone back to the boat. We're leaving."

Hesitantly, they entered the ship and were relieved when it jerked forward and began slowly moving away from the house, the lake-like river and the crystal that continued to hover over it.

"I told you I had something for you." she said, her voice echoing all around them.

They turned to her, watching as she pressed her hands onto the inner walls of her crystal prison. The shimmering stone began to pulsate. A faint hum even seemed to resonate from it. They all watched in a mix of wonder and confusion; even their boat had stopped pulling away.

MATTHEW L. MARTIN

Finally it burst. The crystal shattered into a million little pieces, blanketing their vision with sparkling lights of red and orange, purple and blue, yellow and green…

"Where'd she go?" Jay asked.

The Lady was gone.

The fragments hovered in the air, orbiting around specks of pale blue, which lacked the glow of the rainbow pieces around it. Then all at once, the pieces fell, splashing into the still water below, stirring up a bubbling commotion in the water. "Something's about to happen." Petro said, but you didn't need to be a magi to guess that.

The water erupted a fountain of rainbow colors, spitting out from the jet-stream a silver and blue object. It landed in front of them, sticking out of the ground like a flagpole. It was a glistening sword, wide like Excalibur…with a metal that sparkled with the same iridescent glow of the sword Arthur once drew from the stone throne. It's hilt was blue and it lacked the golden letters on the steel, but other than that it seemed a perfect match.

"A sister sword." the voice whispered to him. "For you, as you set out for…justice."

Eric leaned out of the boat and wrapped his fingers around the blue hilt. A tingle ran through his fingers, from his tips to his spine and up and down his body.

THE LADY IN THE LAKE

The boat jerked forward and once again they were moving, slowly ascending toward the water above them. "Where are we going now?" Jay asked.

"To Rome." Eric replied. That wasn't exactly what Jay was thinking when he asked his question, but it was an effective answer all the same. "We're going to kill the Emperor…and the witch that bends his ear."

MATTHEW L. MARTIN

Appendices

HIGHLIGHTS FROM THE PAST TWENTY YEARS

After Arthur was stabbed and left for dead, Eric picked himself up and confronted the librarian. The small man was not in the mood for talk however; he picked up Excalibur, mumbled something about returning the sword "to where it belongs" and snapped his fingers, whisking Eric away back to Venice. He spent three weeks living in the city, mostly stewing in a mixture of bitterness and anger.

Originally, he planned to make his way back to England, intending to personally deliver the news of Arthur's death to Gwenevere. He began the trek across the Old Lands, but only made it as far as Paris when he received word that the English queen was expecting a royal baby.

Knowing full well that such was impossible, he gave up his desire to return home, choosing instead to remain in Paris to work as hired-muscle for a business man who oversaw a jelly franchise. The job didn't last but it did allow him to meet some shady people, with whom Eric went into business as a mercenary-for-hire.

Whatever shame he felt initially in the new

THE LADY IN THE LAKE

work ended when he encountered a customer on Christmas night, three years after leaving the Library. A Templar Knight was looking to leave his order, on account of the threats his Inquisitor was making against his family. Eric solved his problem, developed a sense of satisfaction in choking the Inquisitor to death, and found a new purpose in the job he originally hated.

It was in that line of work that he met Marcella and with her help found a way to redirect his anger. Along the way they met Petro and Jay, then Fortigo and Dun, and built a network in the French underground to promote their work-for-hire business.

Every now and then news would trickle over from England, about the new boy-King and the mother that everyone assumed ruled in his stead; Eric paid it no mind. That was history. He had a new life and a new purpose and had no desire to be called into any greater quest than a life of light-crime with Marcella at his side.

*****

Gwen struggled, as you might expect, for weeks following the revelation of Lancelot's true identity. Merlin left almost as soon as Kason's body was cold on the floor, leaving her very much pregnant and with the dead body of England's former King lying in front of her. She wrapped his face in a cloth, called for her personal attendants and disposed of the body before anyone could ask too many questions. As far as anyone who knew anything was concerned, Lancelot—not Kason—was dead, Gwen killed him and her child was Arthur's, one day to be King. Only she and Merlin knew the truth.

Though she made no public announcement, it was an open-secret that she killed Lancelot and many of the Camelot staff whispered that perhaps Lancelot had conspired to kill Arthur. The rest of the Kingdom had their own theories, and the more inquisitive Lords went to great lengths to investigate what happened when their Queen returned from her kidnapping.

It did not take much investigating to determine that Gwenevere likely became pregnant after Arthur left to search for the Holy Grail. Once that information was discovered and disseminated around England, murmurs of Mordred's royal legitimacy sprang up. Within a year of his birth, he went from being called "the boy King" to "the bastard King" by less honorable Lords in the land.

Gwen, shrewdly, did not acknowledge or respond to the whispers, preferring to dismiss them as foolish rumors. Without a credible challenger to Mordred's claim and as long as the royal occupants of Camelot were beloved—as Gwen and the young Mordred largely were—there was no practical reason for anyone to risk a Civil War fighting for the throne.

THE LADY IN THE LAKE

Then Scottish rebels sacked the city of Dundee.

Fenial marched an ragtag army north from Sterling and raided the grain storehouses in Dundee. A famine that had plagued the whole northern region of England had seen hundreds die and hundreds more suffer. Despite that, King Mordred did not consent to open the grainhouses and distribute reserves to the Scottish people in need. Without the King's consent, the Scottish Lords were helpless and refused to rebel. Fenial has no such scruples and within a week, the grain was seized, the people were fed and the Scots were in open rebellion.

Skirmishes lasted for a month, with English lawkeepers being sent to arrest Fenial, followed by the lawkeeper's heads being returned to the King. Outright war became inevitable when Fenial crowned himself the first King of the Scots and declared all the land north of York as his own.

Almost immediately thereafter, rumors started stirring that the Irish were negotiating with the rebel King. Despite this, Mordred did not sit down with Fenial to resolve the dispute, nor did he send emissaries to the Irish to secure their non-interference. Though everyone in England believed Gwen to be the actual ruler, she in fact wielded very little control over her son's rash and often ill-considered decisions.

MATTHEW L. MARTIN

The only Knight in his Roundtable he seemed at all interested in hearing was Sir Richard, though his most consistent advice was for the King to yield and prevent a war at all costs; Richard's near-instant affection for the Queen-mother clouded his counsel. The rest of Mordred's Knights of loyalty and counsel were a mix of war mongers and schemers, selected by the young King, not on account of their skill in combat or wisdom, but in flattery.

*****

As for what happened with Merlin, The Lady and others during the intervening two decades… there are answers, but not all answers need to be given. Some are best left unsaid, perhaps to be revealed later. Morgana has been scheming and working to overthrow the Kingdoms of men. The Lady has been scheming and working to undercut Morgana. Pieces are moving into place and all will soon come to ahead.

As you've noticed, no doubt, in previous books, every two stories overlap. The Ill-Winds of Fate and The Headwinds of Destiny take place almost entirely over the same period of time. It's similar in The Quest of Sir Lancelot and The Man with Two Faces, except some events in one book take place before the other book begins, and other events take place after a book ends.

THE LADY IN THE LAKE

This book skips ahead in time a good many years, leaving much to the imagination. That was intentional; time needed to pass to get characters into a different place physically and mentally and allow new characters to be established already by the time this final two-part story begins.

The next book will somewhat take place during the same timeframe as this book, especially early on, but it will also continue beyond where this book ended, as we press toward the conclusion and potential set-up for more(!) books to come. So if you were wondering what's coming next for Gwen, Mordred, Merlin and others, worry not. There is a little more story left to be told in the final volume of **this** Arthur series.

MATTHEW L. MARTIN

STANDARDS AND BANNERS
OF THE KINGDOMS
AND EMPIRES OF THE WORLD
(AS PERTAINING TO THIS BOOK)

ROYAL SIGIL OF KING MORDRED

a white dragon on a field of red

THE LADY IN THE LAKE

SIGIL OF SIR RICHARD

twin crescents on checks of red and green

FLAG OF GRENOBLE

papal cross on a field of red and yellow

MATTHEW L. MARTIN

FLAG OF ISTANBUL

purple moon on a field of grey

SIGIL OF TURKISH HEADHUNTERS

stripes of burgundy, gold and green
with Turkish flower, moon and stars

THE LADY IN THE LAKE

SIGIL OF SIR TERANCE

cross and spur on a shield, over a banner of sky blue

SIGIL OF SIR HANBURY

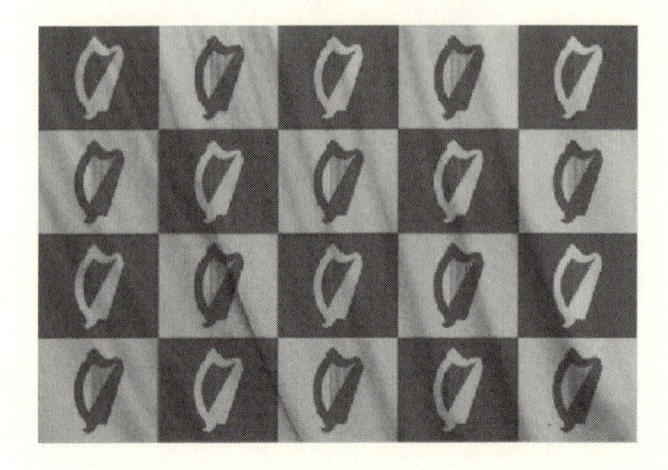

harps on checks of red and gold

MATTHEW L. MARTIN

SIGIL OF SIR OXLEF

*interlocking starburst
on crossing of green and yellow*

FLAG OF YORK

bursts green and blue on a green/blue half-crossing

THE LADY IN THE LAKE

FLAG OF THE UNITED KINGDOM
OF SCOTLAND AND IRELAND

white cross on a royal blue field

MATTHEW L. MARTIN

SIGIL OF BAUDWIN

twin white crescents on a field of cherry red

SIGIL OF LOT

white harp on a field of cherry red

THE LADY IN THE LAKE

CAPITAL OF THE ENGLISH: LONDON
CAPITAL OF THE NORTHERN CELTS: DUBLIN
CAPITAL OF THE NORSE: STOKMYR
CAPITAL OF THE SOUTHERN CELTS: CORONA
CAPITAL OF THE ROMANS: ROME

CAPITAL OF FRANCE: CHAMBORD
CAPITAL OF THE GERMANIANS: GAELGUM
CAPITAL OF THE HOLY LANDS: JERUSALEM
CAPITAL OF THE TURKS: ISTANBUL

MATTHEW L. MARTIN

sand serpents
(terrorize the WuStyni clans)

THE LADY IN THE LAKE

merkall
(drives out the sand snakes)

MATTHEW L. MARTIN

SenTot
(rules the Wustyni)

THE LADY IN THE LAKE

MadSu
(leads a revolution)

MATTHEW L. MARTIN

the lady
(brings Arthur back)

THE LADY IN THE LAKE

raph
(runs a tight bar)

MATTHEW L. MARTIN

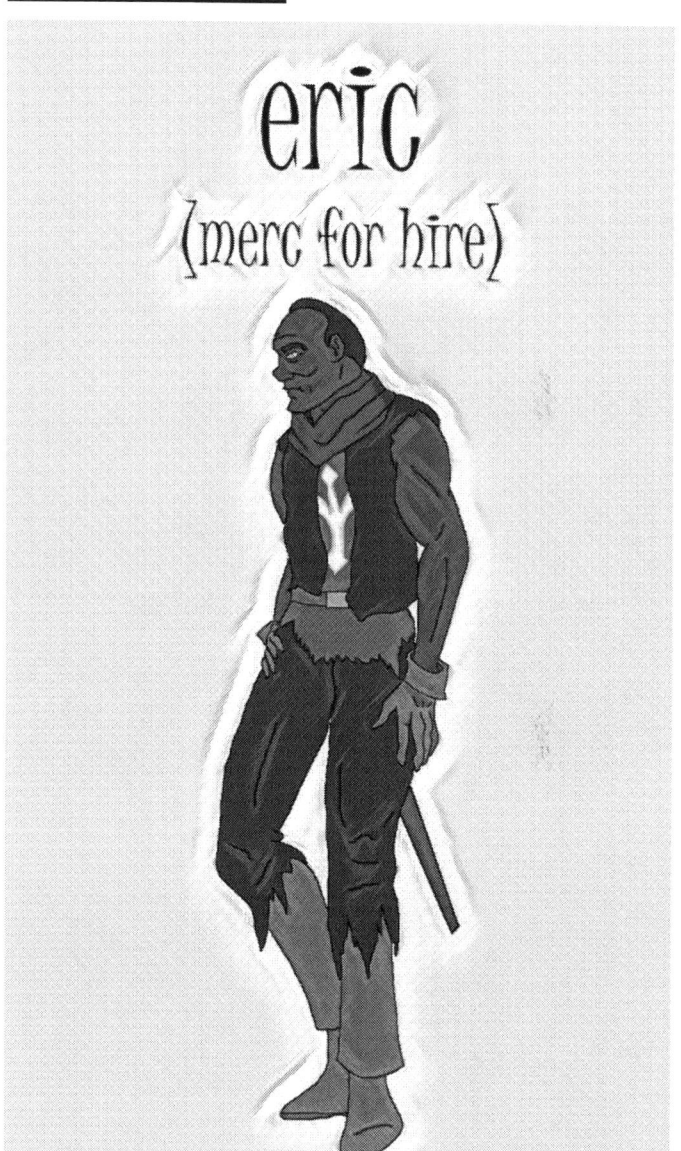

eric
(merc for hire)

THE LADY IN THE LAKE

marcella
(runs Eric's business)

MATTHEW L. MARTIN

jay and petro
(on Eric's team)

THE LADY IN THE LAKE

fortigo and dun
(on Eric's team)

MATTHEW L. MARTIN

O'Mare
(offers Eric a big job)

THE LADY IN THE LAKE

the templar knights
(visit Raph's Bar)

MATTHEW L. MARTIN

mordred
(hates being King)

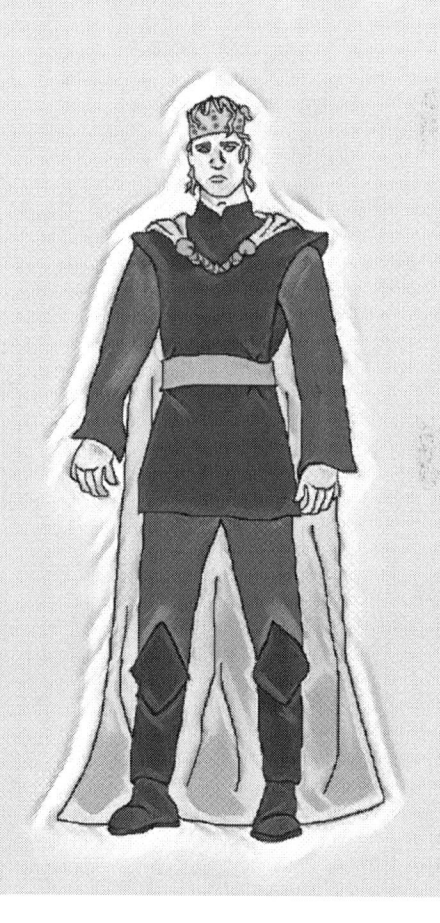

THE LADY IN THE LAKE

sir richard
(tries to mentor the young King)

MATTHEW L. MARTIN

gwenevere
(struggles with grief and motherhood)

THE LADY IN THE LAKE

arthur
(brought back from beyond)

MATTHEW L. MARTIN

corvis
(dislikes The Lady's plan)

THE LADY IN THE LAKE

morgana
(puts her plan in motion)

MATTHEW L. MARTIN

sal
(rides with Eric to Grenoble)

THE LADY IN THE LAKE

morné
(greets Eric and his crew)

MATTHEW L. MARTIN

rumpel
(works his cons)

THE LADY IN THE LAKE

kerem
(gets conned by Rumpel)

MATTHEW L. MARTIN

the beggar
(tangles with Rumpel)

THE LADY IN THE LAKE

merlin
(searches for MadSu)

MATTHEW L. MARTIN

archimedes
(back to tending bar)

THE LADY IN THE LAKE

turkish thugs
(come to collect)

MATTHEW L. MARTIN

the inquisitor
(tangles with Eric and Morné)

THE LADY IN THE LAKE

sir terance
(serves on Mordred's RoundTable)

MATTHEW L. MARTIN

the jailer
(struggles with his conscience)

THE LADY IN THE LAKE

sir hanbury
(serves on Mordred's RoundTable)

MATTHEW L. MARTIN

king fenial
(leads the Scot/Irish rebellion)

THE LADY IN THE LAKE

Sir Oxlef
(betrays Mordred)

MATTHEW L. MARTIN

"king" baudwin
(usurps the throne)

THE LADY IN THE LAKE

lord lot
(claims the English throne for himself)

MATTHEW L. MARTIN

merlin
(escapes from MadSu)

THE LADY IN THE LAKE

MadSu
(hunts down guardians)

MATTHEW L. MARTIN

the genie
(aids in the escape)

THE LADY IN THE LAKE

the inquisitor
(loses the fight...and his clothes)

MATTHEW L. MARTIN

merlin
(searches for The Lady)

THE LADY IN THE LAKE

the lady's house
(under the sea)

MATTHEW L. MARTIN

the man in red and black
(greets Merlin)

THE LADY IN THE LAKE

kilgara
(resides in Camelot's crypt)

MATTHEW L. MARTIN

the lady
(confined to her prison)

THE LADY IN THE LAKE

eric
(starts anew)

MATTHEW L. MARTIN

CONCLUDE THE STORY...
KINGDOM OF ARTHUR
THE DEATH OF ARTHUR

ACKNOWLEDGMENTS

Yes that's supposed to be Braveheart.
It's an homage.

My wife Lauren is an immensely patient woman who has put up with so much from me while I've worked on this. And since this is part five of six…I will continue to be amazed by her patience, understanding and love.

Also there's Phillip who pushed me,
and John who encouraged me,
Eric who humored me,
and…

MATTHEW L. MARTIN

DEDICATION

This one goes to Chris,

who has never failed to be
a sounding board, critic, muse, a humorist.
His insights are rarely anything remarkable,
but rarely also are they are unmemorable.

To my brother in crime.

Made in the USA
Columbia, SC
25 August 2022